Hitchhiker

To Janice,
Good to meet
you at JSF

Enjoy

Bob

12-9-17

HITCHHIKER

STORIES FROM THE KENTUCKY HOMEFRONT

BOB THOMPSON

FOREWORD BY
ROBERTA SIMPSON BROWN

Scholarly publisher for the Commonwealth,
serving Bellarmine University, Berea College, Centre College of Kentucky, Eastern Kentucky University, The Filson Historical Society, Georgetown College, Kentucky Historical Society, Kentucky State University, Morehead State University, Murray State University, Northern Kentucky University, Transylvania University, University of Kentucky, University of Louisville, and Western Kentucky University.

Editorial and Sales Offices: The University Press of Kentucky
663 South Limestone Street, Lexington, Kentucky 40508-4008
www.kentuckypress.com

Cataloging-in-Publication data available from the Library of Congress

ISBN 978-0-8131-7428-0 (hardcover : alk. paper)
ISBN 978-0-8131-7430-3 (epub)
ISBN 978-0-8131-7429-7 (pdf)

This book is printed on acid-free paper meeting the requirements of the American National Standard for Permanence in Paper for Printed Library Materials.

Manufactured in the United States of America.

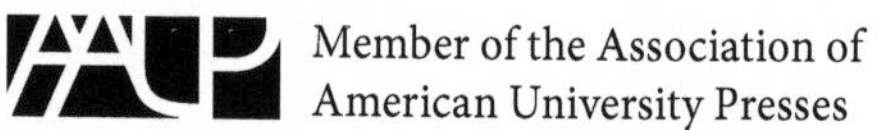

Contents

Foreword

Except for the author, I am probably the person most excited about the publication of this book! Bob Thompson and I have been friends and coworkers at the Corn Island Storytelling Festival for many years. During that time, Bob wrote and told story after story at the festival and for the *Kentucky Homefront* radio show. It became obvious that this was a man who never ran out of stories. He did not have to tell other people's stories, nor did he have to repeat his own.

He always had time to encourage and support the rest of us storytellers. He introduced me on a program once as "The Queen of the Cold-Blooded Tales," a phrase my publisher liked so much that he used it as the title of my second book. Bob's creativity, even in introductions, shows no limit.

Bob has many professional titles of his own: engineer, storyteller, writer, event producer, Kentucky Colonel, self-appointed "Commissioner of Kentucky Front Porches," and "Resident Front Porch Philosopher" on his weekly National Public Radio show.

His stories cover a wide range of subjects, including ghosts, humor, sadness, inspiration, and personal experiences, that paint a vivid picture of his Western Kentucky roots. I wonder if the nearby Ohio and

Mississippi Rivers had some magical effect on him as he was growing up. His stories seem to flow endlessly like the rivers themselves.

Many of us Kentuckians can identify with Bob's childhood experiences, which often parallel our own. We remember working in the fields and visits to old country stores, where we listened with great interest to stories of the old folk who came as customers and stayed awhile to visit.

In most homes, after dinner was over and chores were done, family and neighbors gathered to share stories, often about ghosts. These were the times when the dead were remembered, or when they returned to bring a message or merely to say hello. Bob has taken special care to pass these stories on to future generations. Even if the reader doesn't believe in ghosts, these encounters will endure in the mind. Images are embedded in my memory of Bob hanging tobacco, helping with crop planting, and realizing that his long-dead grandfather was still watching over him. Bob makes his front porch ghosts as real as an ordinary visit from a friend.

Bob never writes ghost stories to shock or scare readers. His style is to tell the story in a matter-of-fact, believable manner. Using carefully chosen details, he pulls readers into the experience, allowing them to feel what the characters are feeling and then come to their own conclusions about what has happened. These stories can certainly send shivers surging through the body, but they can also touch the heart and open the mind to the presence of the supernatural. He doesn't tell you what to think or attempt to convince you to become a believer in ghosts if you don't believe already. His presentation makes his stories suitable for family reading and for people of all ages.

I began telling Bob he should write a book after hearing other people tell him the same thing, but he kept putting it off. I increased my urging after my husband Lonnie and I were repeatedly asked at our book signings if we had any stories about Western Kentucky. We had only a few that we had heard from relatives or neighbors, but I kept thinking about Bob's wealth of stories not yet in book form. What a shame it would be if those stories went unprinted and were lost to us forever!

I cranked my urging up to the level of nagging. I knew there was a market waiting for his Western Kentucky stories, but I also knew these same stories had universal appeal and power. These were stories for everybody.

Maybe he got tired of hearing nagging from me and others, or maybe the time was just right, but Bob finally decided to send a manuscript to the acquisitions editors at the University Press of Kentucky. At last, the right author met the right publisher, and *Hitchhiker: Stories from the Kentucky Homefront* became a reality. After all these years, the book I had hoped for is now in print.

What happens next? *Hitchhiker* offers something for everyone. It can be read for fun and excitement or used to study the way these stories reflect our culture and history. Readers will become a part of Kentucky's storytelling community and traditional heritage. This book is likely to make its way into folklore archives and give future readers a clear picture of some of our most treasured traditions.

This is a book that readers should buy, enjoy, and keep on a shelf for future use. Be sure to leave room for more books to come. Bob Thompson is not a one-book author and he is not limited to writing ghost stories. I expect there will soon be more delightful books by Bob on many aspects of life. We readers will be better for reading them. I know I am ready and waiting.

Roberta Simpson Brown
Author / Storyteller

Introduction

Our lives, all of them, are alluvial landscapes, shaped by the streams of energy flowing around and through us, eroding and replenishing.

This book is a fictional memoir, arranged in roughly chronological order, of the author's passage through time, which began in this iteration at Riverside Hospital in Paducah, Kentucky, on the banks of the Ohio, in the midst of currents flowing since before light and breath.

The perspective of this book is that our seemingly time-linear lives flow mostly on one side of a fragile, sometimes transparent veil, separating us from other dimensions, realities, and entities, all part of the same flow. These stories are meant as my witness to the conversations, artifacts, and energies flowing through that veil. From any single-dimensional perspective, these stories might seem "beyond reality," and from that viewpoint, of course they are.

The first six stories of this book, and the last, are centered at my family's country grocery store, in the small rural community of Ragland, at the western edge of McCracken County, a mile from the Ballard County line, in the Ohio River floodplain of

Kentucky's Jackson Purchase Region. They retrace my early wanderings along its roads, rivers, and lakes, often unconscious of the deep and rich spirit world that abounds there. All the stories and their characters have real connections to locations, artifacts, and family—the currents, objects, and personalities that flowed through my youth.

Location

Far Western Kentucky, where I spent my first eighteen years, has a dual archeological and physiographical personality that can be correctly considered to be part of both the lower Ohio River Valley and the Lower Mississippi Valley. What is not as ambiguous is that the rich delta land lies at the greatest confluence of rivers in North America, where all the flows come together.

The Tennessee and Cumberland Rivers empty into the Ohio just before it goes around the big sweeping curve called Monkey's Eyebrow and empties into the much smaller (30 percent smaller) Mississippi at Cairo, Illinois. There is nothing about far Western Kentucky that is not connected with its rivers.

The Ohio and its many tributaries were the main arteries of the young nation, through which the commerce of the republic flowed. If the river was the original superhighway of its day, then its many landings were its truck stops and logistics depots. Many roads of the area still bear the names of their termini, either at nineteenth-century riverboat landings or at one of the many oxbow lakes spawned by the river: Carrico, Ogden, and Joppa Landings, or Crawford, Turner, and Shelby Lakes.

Many of the narrow old farm roads are named after the ancestors of families who came down the river, settled, and still live there: House, Helm, Warford, Matlock, Grief, Reid, Vaughn, and Lanier. Each one recalls a face, a story, and a ghost.

Family

My history is inextricably and mystically linked with the river. My Great-Great-Grandfather Starks died in 1864 at Fort Anderson, on the banks of the Ohio River, during the Battle of Paducah; eighty-six years later, I was born at that exact spot, in Riverside Hospital, built over the foundations of the old fort. My father's family came down the Ohio from Virginia after the Revolution.

My mother's father was taken by the swollen river when I was a year and a half old; his mother's family had come up the Mississippi from New Orleans after crossing from Le Havre, France.

Except for my mom, all the women in my early life were widows. I did not have the privilege of knowing a single grandfather or great-grandfather; they were beyond the veil before my second spring. I always had the feeling that all of them were somehow with me, watching, whispering, protecting, keeping me from their mistakes. I am an amalgamation of them all. I have many of their physical and emotional attributes: deep-set eyes, big veins in my arms and hands, square jaw, thick and early grey hair, as well as their mannerisms, demeanor, and general goodwill. The physical similarities are confirmed by pictures; the personality traits were frequently referenced by relatives and reinforced through a plethora of surrogate grandfathers, lifelong friends of my forebears whom I've long suspected of having sworn some secret oath to my elders to take a hand in my education. These aged local denizens lectured around the Warm Morning Stove in the winter and on the sheltered front porch bench the rest of the year. Whereas grandmothers are often uncomfortable offering up memories and stories of their dead spouses, the old guys on the porch, safely out of earshot of the widows, exhibited no such reticence. The truth was always told on the porch!

In compensation for my lack of male elders, I was blessed with good timing and a full complement of grandmothers and great-grandmothers. To say that I had a close connection with each of them would be an understatement.

The day after I turned ten, Great-Grandma Thompson started the tradition of departing near my birthday, a tradition that three of the remaining five grandmothers would honor. The nearly annual event had a sobering effect on my birthday celebrations, my psyche, and my understanding of timing and other realities. These departures did not come to me cushioned as after-the-fact news from afar; they unfolded as up-close, day-by-day transitions of dear childhood friends. Only one of them did not spend her last months next door at Granny Parker's house or across the road from the grocery in the little block house we called the Grandma House.

From all my ancestors I have a vast treasure of the things that carry their spirit, the instruments of their daily lives: rings, snuff boxes, biscuit cutters, branding irons, hand tools, horse bits, doilies, and quilt frames, to name just a few. I listen to their voices almost daily through their letters, diaries, recipes, and notes in the margins of books and Bibles. I sleep under their quilts and mark the passing of time by shadows and the chiming of their clocks. I open all the blinds and walk around my house in window light, navigating in the evenings by their lamps to understand their world, their light. I shave with their brushes and straight razors and carry their pocket knives and watches. I sew on their old Singer machines and talk to them across time. All are my loving guardian angels.

Travels

You may consider chapters 7–16 of this book my traveling ghost show. My ghosts have always traveled with me, saving me from precarious situations naively blundered into. These stories are walkabouts, spirit quests, adventures on paths where spirits might be expected but are still always surprising and harrowing; the interactions depend on which of my spiritual allies and guardian angels were on duty at a given moment.

At eighteen, I started weaning myself from Western Kentucky. Having a proclivity for literature, science, and tinkering, I was fortunate to get a small physics scholarship from the operators of the Paducah Gaseous Diffusion (atomic) Plant, and went off to the Purchase's only major university, Murray State, coming home in the summers to earn spending money. Murray had yet to offer a degree in my chosen field, engineering, so after my sophomore year I transferred to the University of Kentucky and permanently moved away from Ragland, though never away from the river.

I'm not sure where I got my penchant for travel; perhaps it was the pictures and stories from a treasured 1952 set of the *World Book Encyclopedia* that has been with me since before memory, or the fact that the only long trip my family ever took was a week-long car ride with three other families to Pensacola, Florida. More likely it is the spirit of the river in me, always on the move. Whatever it was, I have an insatiable wanderlust, a quest for exploration and alternative perspective that has endured my entire life.

That ever-moving spirit and perspective has often led to other dimensions, and encounters with their resident entities. Despite being open to the possibility, such a transport or meeting is almost always disconcerting both initially and in retrospect. Afterward, it becomes unnerving when the notion starts to seep into your consciousness that the encounter was likely not happenstance, that you and the ghost have for years been on a collision course, foreordained, inevitable, and maybe even necessary. Scarier still is the realization that your reaction to an encounter might be the result of a lesson from a dream . . . or a previous incarnation!

Finally, let me address one remaining issue. I am surprised and confused by the paltry amount of ghost stories from the area in which I grew up; after all, it is not without a history that would seem likely to spawn such stories. The mysterious Mississippians inhabited it so long ago and disappeared so thoroughly that the Native Americans living in the area when Europeans came, the Chickasaw, had no knowledge of them. It would seem logical that there should be spirit remnants of them wandering about, but there appears to be a protective screen between us and their stories, their knowledge. There are of course many isolated instances of untimely deaths, murders, and lynchings that one would expect to birth ghosts, but few have come forward with those stories.

There were at least two racially motivated lynchings in Ballard County around the turn of the twentieth century. C. J. Miller, an African American accused of murdering two white girls, was tortured and lynched by an angry mob in Wickliffe despite the protestations of the girls' father, who claimed the killer was a white man. A decade later, Tom Hall, accused of wounding a white man, was similarly dragged from his jail cell and lynched. Cairo, Illinois, at the confluence of the Ohio and Mississippi, has a long history of racial violence, perhaps best illustrated by the 1967 case of a nineteen-year-old soldier, Robert Hunt, who was found hanged in the local police station while home on leave. The incident was ruled a suicide.

Of course, I am making one personal and purposeful omission; it pains me that when I type the name of my and my parents' high school, Heath, into any intuitive search engine, it supplies the word *shooting* before I can finish typing. I have far too many connections to families on both sides of that tragedy to make comment. Those ghosts are not for me to deal with.

Otherwise, the eight Kentucky counties comprising the Jackson Purchase seem to have been shielded from the massive loss of life that often breeds ghosts. All the big battles of the Western Theater of the Civil War were fought just outside its boundaries. The blood of five hundred Union soldiers of African descent, shot as they tried to surrender at Fort Pillow, stained the Mississippi for two hundred yards, but that was far downriver in Tennessee. The battles at Fort Donelson and Fort Henry, on the Cumberland and Tennessee Rivers respectively, were also in Tennessee. The closest river disaster was when the USS *Essex* lost thirty-two sailors on the Tennessee River after a Confederate cannonball struck her boiler.

In contrast, Grant crossed the Ohio at Paducah in 1861 on the longest pontoon bridge of the war without casualties, and the Battle of Paducah in 1864 had less than fifty dead—but they did include my great-great-grandfather, inside the fort, and Colonel Albert P. Thompson, a hometown boy whose bad timing and slacker angel allowed him to position his head at the same intersection of time and space as a Union cannonball. The only casualities of the Black Patch Tobacco War at the beginning of the twentieth century were tobacco barns, warehouses, and plant beds. Even the massive 1811 New Madrid Earthquake, estimated to be the largest ever in North America, which created Reel Foot Lake and made the Mississippi flow backward, is known to have killed only one person, in Missouri.

My own theory on this general lack of human carnage and its resultant dearth of lingering spirits is that the area is sacred, preserved by some divine intervention as the critical pumping heart of the continent. To encounter spirits in this unique area requires fortuitous timing, because the departed energies of their souls cannot long linger. Even those trapped in the dark sloughs or those with reason and intent to tarry are eventually flushed out, down to the great combining seas where they are evaporated, reconstituted, and recycled back into the flow.

River Watch

Outside it was foggy, damp, and cold. Inside, the family was warm and drowsy, just settled into the living room after a big Sunday dinner. In my grandfather's lap, my attention was on the tick-tocky, shiny thingy swinging in front of me: his pocket watch, a recent birthday present from Granny.

The protective feelings and the softly whispered promises he made to this vulnerable little life in his arms had overwhelmed him with energy and spurred his already industrious spirit toward new plans. It was one of those plans that even in this tender moment he couldn't keep his mind away from—the task that had to be done today, before the early dark, rain or not. After three weeks, the constant rain had finally stopped, but at any moment it was likely to begin again, and he needed to get to the river bottoms and check that lumber.

At the cost of several sons, the last world war had made Ohio River landing communities prosperous; now Korea and the Cold War promised continued growth and loss. Eight miles away, toward Paducah, the government was building a gigantic nuclear enrichment facility. Securing the support of the Illinois congressional delegation meant the atomic plant's massive electricity needs would be met with a new generating facility in Joppa, Illinois, straight down at the end of our road, three miles away across the river.

Granddad's Ogden Landing Road country grocery was on a direct path between the two behemoth construction projects and as close to the Ohio River's 1937 high-water mark as insurance would allow. Business was good; every available shack, trailer, spare room, and campground in the area was rented to accommodate the influx of workers.

The tallest power line–transmission towers in the world, half-sized Eiffel Towers, were being built on the banks of the Ohio, three in each state. The methods, machinery, and progress of these marvels of technology were the objects of many local family sightseeing trips to the river. Massive, silo-sized concrete cylinders stuck thirty feet high out of the sandy river bank and were buried farther below, each anchoring a single foot of each tower's four legs.

Grandfather marveled at how much wood it had taken to construct the concrete forms for just one of those things. He calculated that each base contained enough wood to build a good-sized family home.

The construction manager for the concrete contractor was a customer at the grocery, and soon Granddad had a deal: after the concrete cured, if he supplied the labor to dismantle and haul the wooden forms away, he could keep the lumber. With a young partner to share half the work and get an equal share of lumber, he figured there would be enough material in his part to frame two houses next to the store, one for himself and Granny, and one for his daughter, son-in-law, and the not-yet-two-year-old grandson he held in his lap.

In the cozy living room, I finally grew drowsy and went to

sleep on his chest, to the tick-tock of the pocket watch clutched in my hand. Gently, he got up and took me into the bedroom, laying me in the crib before carefully wiggling the watch from my grasp and kissing me goodbye. In the living room he kissed Granny, put on his hip boots and rain gear, and headed to the river bottoms.

Three weeks earlier, just as it started raining, he and Bill had finished removing the wood from the concrete, but not before the rain-soaked river bottom roads had become too soft to haul it out to dryer land. Now the river was so high that the priority was to keep the lumber from washing down to Cairo and on to New Orleans.

Granddad and Bill had lashed the piles of wood together with cables and chains, anchoring them to the new and barely cured concrete piers. This afternoon it was his turn to take the boat more than a mile through the backwater to check the bundles to make sure their investment was still secure.

My last living grandfather got in his jeep and drove off into the thick, wet fog.

I grew up in one of the new houses Grandfather had envisioned, built not with the lumber he went to get, but with the life insurance money Grandmother got after his drowning.

My mother, fearing and hating the river for taking his spirit without the decency to give back his body, never went near the river again.

As is often the case, a parent's greatest fear becomes a child's greatest love. I grew up with a peculiar affinity for the river and the dark forested solitude of what we called the river bottoms. It seemed that every spare moment of my early teenage years was spent wandering through those deep woods. Stories of stealthy panthers, slimy reptiles, and river ghosts didn't diminish the strange sense of kinship I had for the river and its surroundings. I spent day after day wandering its vast uninhabited forests, dotted with oxbow lakes and dark sloughs, where the sun never got a chance to expose or dry out its secret hiding places in the wet, soggy ground.

Early fall found me fishing along the sandy river bank across from the Joppa Steam Plant, just downstream from one of the big towers. On one of those days, I noticed a small section of something protruding from a large jumbled pile of driftwood accumulated amongst a thick cluster of water maples and sycamores. Careful of lurking cottonmouth moccasins while picking through the jumble, I started untangling the pile. Finally, I could see what it was: an old but reasonably intact wooden john boat.

Wow! I thought.

I knew Mom would never let me have a boat, so this had to remain my secret. I studied the details of marine construction from the fishing boats in Crawford Lake and in my set of the *World Book Encyclopedia*, and over the following weeks I was able to sneak enough hand tools, wood, hardware, and caulk to the bottoms on my motorcycle to return my hidden treasure to seaworthiness.

I spent many glorious autumn days floating down the river in my secret barge. It felt so right, so relaxing to be on the water in that boat. Often, I would paddle upstream next to the shore, up beyond the middle tower, before pushing out into the current and drifting back downstream, often napping with my fishing line tied to my toe. Huck Finn had nothing on me.

I idled away the afternoons and Saturdays of that late warm fall in secret boyhood bliss, until one idyllic day when a sudden bump woke me from my drifting daydreams. I looked up to see Bill Wallace's startled look, staring down at me from the fishing boat now alongside me.

Bill was our local commercial fisherman, who people said "knew the river better than anyone." He could catch fish when no one else could. Not a braggart without foundation, Bill claimed to know every sandbar, snag, and current on the Ohio between the Tennessee and the Mississippi. To my relief, and despite considerable mental workings that showed in his face, Bill didn't say a word to me, nor I to him. He just nodded, released his hold on my boat, and drifted away, back to checking his nets.

I've been discovered! The secret will be out! My river days are over!

Every day I expected the hammer to fall on my playhouse, but it never came. Bill didn't tell.

Feeling increasingly safe in the comfort of my continuing secret, I began to let myself get excited about the arrival of the country boy Holy Grail of the wetlands: goose hunting season. On scouting trips to the bottoms, I started camouflaging the boat, cutting willow branches and arranging them so that the boat looked like a floating tree snag or a small island.

I was bursting with excitement as late November approached. The weather was ideal for a great hunting season. The rains came on the first of November and the river started rising, covering the river bottoms' corn fields, making it ideal for the large flocks of Canadian geese migrating down the Mississippi Flyway to land and feed on the leftover harvest in the flooded fields.

I checked on my boat regularly, moving it farther and farther back each day to keep the rising water from swamping it.

The night before the season began, I was sitting in the back of Granny's store by the big Warm Morning Stove, cleaning and oiling my shotgun, when Bill came in the front door.

Oh, no, please God, not now!

He got a cold soda out of the box at the front of the store and came back to sit by the stove. He nodded to me.

"Gonna try 'em in the morning?"

"Hope to," I said, pleading with my eyes for him not to spill the beans here on the eve of my greatest adventure. He seemed to understand as he glanced toward Granny.

It wasn't long before Granny got up from her chair and headed toward the front of the store to restock the cold-drink box, her signal to any lingering customers that the store was about to close. Bill's eyes followed until she was out of hearing distance, not taking his eyes off her. Then he started.

"You know, son, your grandpa was a fine man. Me and him spent many a day together, working and fishing and hunting them woods . . . and when I hit a rough spot, he let me run up a pretty big tab at the store, a bill that would have scared most people to death. He knew I'd pay him when I had it. He understood people and . . . he understood that river, son."

He paused for a moment.

"Ain't nobody knows that river better than me, son, and I'm telling you, there's strange things that goes on when that old river gets loose and spills its banks. There's nobody that can explain what goes on down there in that fog when the water gets up in them lakes and sloughs and lets them spirits loose! There's things in them backwaters can suck you right down, like a big old snapping turtle coming up under a young duck."

He hesitated before he went on.

"I've seen and heard riverboats out there in the fog, big boats that I know'd sunk twenty years ago. With my own eyes, I've seen old hulls go by . . . with skeletons as deck hands."

He fixed on my eyes, gauging my reaction.

"I ain't lying, son! Some folks say there's spirits living in the black mud of them sloughs, things that only get free when the river gets over 'em. Whatever you think you know about that river, you don't know enough. You just be careful, son, cause if that ole river wants you, it'll take you, just like it took your grandpa . . . and outta that same boat."

The last part exploded in my head. *What? That same boat!*

Before I could ask for an explanation, Granny finished refilling the drink box for tomorrow's customers and headed back toward us. Bill got up, said "Night, ma'am" to Granny, and headed for the front door, followed closely by me. He paused at the door, turning back to me.

"You be careful tomorrow, son!"

I slept little that night thinking about Bill's unsettling revelation. *Have I found my grandfather's boat—the one he died in? What does THAT mean?*

I was up and gone on my motorcycle hours before dawn the next morning, to what my family believed was a day of hunting along the edges of the backwater. Muddy roads, drizzle, and the wall of white fog, inches from my nose, slowed my progress to a crawl. The closer I got to the river, the more mindful I became that I was experiencing exactly what Granddad had on that afternoon in his jeep. Was I was reliving his last day on earth? I would try to be as careful as I knew how!

The river, growing all night, had crept a good quarter of a mile up the road from the day before. Taking my best guess how much it might continue to rise while I was hunting, I parked the bike that distance away and walked back to the water's edge. Wading through the deepening water, holding my gun chest-high and trying to stay on the high ground of the submerged road, I wasn't sure if my hip boots were going to be tall enough for me to reach the spot where I had left the boat the evening before. In the last bit of cloudy light, I had pulled the boat up on dry land; as a precaution, I had tied it to a tree more than three feet above the ground. Now the rope was barely above the water. With dark water lapping at the top of my boots, I placed my gun across the seats and carefully climbed up into the old boat, untied it, and started paddling blindly through the dark, flooded woods above the sunken roadbed.

The fog was so claustrophobically thick that I could see no more than two feet in any direction. I navigated from one ghostly tree shadow to another, fighting against the swirling current, along the edge of the old road carved through the woods. When I crossed the slough at the end of Crawford Lake, I thought of what Bill had said. For long, sensory-challenged moments, filled only by dark images and my internal debate, the water lapped at the boat, swirling beneath me in eerie quietness. Something dark and unseen was about to suck me under. I knew it.

I concentrated on my plan. I was going to make my way through the woods to the center tower. Once there, I would reorient myself and push out into the flow. From previous scouting, I knew a flock of geese almost always roosted among some big willow trees a short distance downstream. My plan was to lie down in the boat, hidden by the willow branches, and drift unnoticed into the midst of the gaggle, arriving at first light, the moment when it's legal to begin shooting. I had no doubt that it would take only a few exciting seconds of furious, honking, wet-wing flapping and shotgun blasts for me to take the legal bag limit of Canadians.

But I had to get there first. Back in the boat, I was near total panic, hopelessly lost and ready to abandon this creepy nonsense, when suddenly, just a few feet away, something huge loomed over me out the mist. Startled and on edge, I jerked and nearly capsized the boat before realizing . . . it was one of the four giant concrete piers at the base of the tower. I was exactly where I wanted to be, underneath the middle tower.

My nerves, now somewhat sedated by the familiar, allowed me to reorient. Squinting through the dense fog, I finally located the tops of submerged willow trees that marked a path out onto the river. After long moments of palpitating trepidation, I finally pushed off the hard concrete pier, out into the soft white void of sensory deprivation. I couldn't see willow tops anymore.

I must be out in the river.

I tried desperately to focus my heightened senses, but for the life of me I couldn't tell which direction I was drifting. I hoped, I prayed, that I was drifting downstream, not out into the river, into the shipping channel near the Illinois side.

For lengthy minutes I strained to hear the sound of the geese I wanted to be approaching. I tried to get my bearings by listening for the normally loud roar of the Joppa Steam Plant across the river, but all was strangely silent.

I was near to a panicked scream, but thought, *What good would that do? What would I do after screaming?* I was in this and there was no turning back!

I became more disoriented than I had ever been in my young life. One moment I would think the Kentucky side of the river was "over there," then it would change. *Am I in an eddy? A whirlpool?* The fog was like cotton; it blocked out all sound and light. I was in an alien world where I had no sense of sight or direction, only muffled sound. It was like floating in outer space. I began to feel a spinning sensation . . . I WAS spinning! I gave up any hope of salvaging the hunt and started to paddle, but I couldn't determine which direction to go to reach safety.

Then I heard it: the rumble of a big engine. I frantically turned to determine its direction. I paddled furiously one way before changing my mind and reversing. It was getting louder and closer.

Images flashed through my mind for some rational explanation, some reassurance. Big barges did not normally travel out of the channel, on this side of the river. *CRAP! What am I thinking? The river is twenty feet over flood stage! They could run in any part of the river they want! SHIT!*

I was going to be run over by a barge. They'd never see me, and if they did it would be too late. Maybe it was one of Bill's ghost ships, looking for me. Either way, I was going to die in this boat, just like my grandfather.

The sound got louder and louder till it was almost on top of me. My heart thundered in my ears as the running lights finally came rushing at me through the fog, bearing down from above. I knew, real or imagined, I was about to be run over, chewed up, and sucked under like a waterlogged leaf. I grabbed a paddle and started digging at the river as the roar of the engine and the splashing of water filled my consciousness.

"AHHHH!" A scream, from somewhere, maybe me, split the fog, as the towering dark shadow of the bow, blocking all else out, came for me quickly out of the mist. I felt an overpowering surge of energy.

The next sound I heard was water slapping against something. The sun had burned away some of the fog, and I was lying in the bottom of the boat. *In an after-life?* I wondered. I raised my head, expecting angels, or worse, and looked about me. The boat rested on a high sand bar, on some shore I didn't recognize. I lay back trying to figure out if I was alive. *Did I go to sleep in the boat and have a dream?* Then I heard another noise, a tick-tock coming from beside my head. I jerked around and there on the boat seat beside my head was that gold pocket watch.

Lucy

By the time I had any sense of reality, my widowed grandmother was the very busy sole proprietor of a prospering country grocery store. Sunday dinner was the only family meal that Granny had time to cook anymore, and often she had to give up morning services at Newton Creek Baptist church to accomplish that.

There were five of us most Sundays: Granny, Mom, Dad, me, and Granny's ninety-two-year-old mother and housemate, Grandma Lucy.

Unless there was company, Grandfather's chair at the head of the table, in front of the window, stayed empty.

Mom and Dad sat on one side with their backs to the wall, below Grandad's picture. Grandma Lucy and Granny sat facing the picture with their backs to the kitchen. This arrangement accommodated Grandma Lucy's wheelchair and gave Granny better access to wait the table from the kitchen. I sat on the end, between Grandma Lucy and Mom, looking out past Granddad's empty chair into the back yard, wondering if Grandma's ghosts were looking in at us.

I was an intelligent and curious child, benefiting from being an only child and from having seasoned store patrons as best friends and playmates. My education began long before school age, and by the time I started first grade I was already considered “smart.” I was well ahead of most of the other fifth graders, but this Sunday I was still not smart enough to go ahead and eat the strange speckled butter beans on my plate, despite repeated encouragements from Mom. I was just smart enough to closely monitor Dad’s reaction, waiting for him to weigh in with the final say. I could sense it coming, he was about to fix eyes on me and render judgment, when Great-Grandma Lucy spoke up first and said, “Robert, I love them butter beans. You’ll like ’em too. I know!”

Grandma was buying me time and giving me gentle guidance, but smart eleven-year-old boys are touchy about advice from anyone, especially a ninety year old who has begun to see dead people in her bedroom and invisible people in the yard. Her unwelcome intervention and suspect mentality did not sit well with me, nor did, in my educated opinion, her inaccurate use of the word “love.”

I tersely replied, “Grandma, I don’t love anything! I like a lot of things, but I don’t LOVE anything!”

The moment the words were out of my mouth, I was ashamed. In the long, reflective silence, I did not look up to the frowns I knew were there.

Until I was eight, Grandma Lucy lived at Grahamville with my great-aunt Evey, her oldest surviving daughter. Every Sunday after services, we’d drive the ten miles to her house for dinner. It was just what we did.

One August Sunday near my birthday, as we were leaving, Granny leaned in close to Grandma Lucy’s ear and, for the three-hundredth time, repeated her usual farewell: “We have to go now, Mom. Why don’t you just come on home with me and stay awhile?”

It was well known that Grandma Lucy was never hesitant to make a judgment call and follow through with it, but it still shocked everyone when she nodded and said, "Yes, I think I will."

Before anyone could process another word, she was up, hobbling around on her crutches, gathering her entire worldly possessions of three dresses and a gown into a brown paper bag. With a little stunned help, she was seated in the back of the Pontiac with me.

The import of the moment was not clear to me, but everyone else knew; she had chosen where she would spend her last days. I was just excited at the prospect of a new neighbor.

Six days a week, Granny was busy from morning till night at the grocery. Grandma Lucy's limited mobility meant she would be alone at the house most of the day. The grocery was already home to the only TV in the community, but now Granny purchased another RCA black-and-white to entertain Gramdma Lucy.

This modern upgrade had huge implications for Grandma Lucy and for me. She was seldom alone while Granny was next door running the grocery; we were both mesmerized by the new technology.

It became a routine for me to sleep over at Granny's on Friday nights so I did not run the risk of missing a moment of Saturday morning cartoons. Grandma Lucy and I spent the day watching *Looney Tunes*, *Popeye*, *Donald & Mickey*, *My Friend Flicka*, Roy Rogers, Dale Evans, Gene Autry, *Captain Kangaroo*, *Little Rascals*, and *Winky Dink and You*. Later in the day, we'd watch PeeWee Reese and Dizzy Dean's *Game of the Week* on the black-and-white wonder box.

I would set the channel and volume before perching my skinny bottom on the wide flat armrest of Grandma's spacious oak rocking chair, leaning back into her shoulder and waiting for her arm to come around me. For hours we would watch the magic screen together.

I noticed that she started dressing differently, wearing her best housecoats over her gown. When I asked her about it, she said, "Because that nice man [Art Linkletter] waves to me when he sees me every day, and I wave back."

Differences in age and life experience didn't keep us from becoming best friends. I began to absorb some of Grandma Lucy's memories of a different world and a different time. She had seen the transition from candlelight to kerosene and then to electricity; she was older than screen doors, sliced bread, and automobiles. She had never lived in a house that she owned. She used strange words like *partridges*, *Jennie and a Jack*, *dominiker*, *fracas*, *fortnight*, *shoat*, *dropsey*, and *kilter*.

In short, Grandma was a dear old soul, and the error of my ways at the dinner table made my head hang heavy in the hushed silence. I usually loved listening to her stories from another world. I wondered, *Why am I being such a little snot to her today? What did I know of love to be lecturing her!*

I was not anxious to meet her gaze, but finally, when the excruciating silence made me chance a glance, I realized she was not staring at me at all. She had a far-off expression on her face. She was somewhere else.

It was 1890 and twenty-year-old Lucy was on her knees in the garden, sobbing, crying big tears from a deep-welled place. The crying became a family chorus as the newborn slung on her breast, the scared two-year-old daughter, and a rambunctious three-year-old son at the edge of the garden joined their voices to the boo-hooing. Her drunken husband, passed out in the front yard, was the only one unperturbed.

Life was pressing down hard on Lucy and she felt old. The weight of the world was heavy on her young shoulders as she stared down at the ground, thinking that to be buried beneath it would be easier. Long gone were the exciting days when a fifteen-year-old Marshall County girl had climbed up on the buckboard wagon seat beside her new husband and started out on what seemed like a grand adventure.

The journey to the isolated tenant farmhouse was a tortuously long, bumpy, three-day wagon trip over rutted and washed-out dirt roads that jarred the baby, blue and dead, out of her.

That seemed like a lifetime ago. Now her days were filled with never-ending cooking, washing, gardening, canning, sewing, fieldwork, and kids. Jonah had been born a day before her sixteenth birthday, and then Lola and then baby Emmitt.

Her husband, John, the spoiled child of a Union cavalry officer dead at Paducah days after his son's second birthday, was much more fond of strong drink than work. The kids went through the last winter with worn-out shoes because John had taken their share of the tobacco money and gone to town—always a dangerous proposition for a man prone to strong drink. He had bought the shoes, but somehow lost them in a night of revelry, and came home broke and empty handed.

She could not have felt more alone, abandoned, and without love. There were no more tears, only sobs, as Lucy stared down at the ground at the new spring sprouts of butter beans just breaking through the dirt. She smiled weakly; she did love those beans. They were speckled, the special family seeds her mother had given her on the day she left home, enough to plant that first garden.

Loving memories flooded back. In an instant, Lucy knew the real problem. It was not a lack of love. Her children loved her, and even John, in his own way, loved her. But there was little solace in any of that. She knew that love was all but dead in her since that poor baby was buried under the chestnut tree without a name or even a marker.

Like a bolt of lightning, it hit her. That was it! She saw the problem clearly now, and the solution was hers alone. It was all up to her. It had always been! But could she ever love again and risk it being taken away? She looked down at the beans poking through the ground between her knees. Maybe. She did love those beans with the speckled places on them. They had been passed down through the family for generations. Yes, she loved them and she loved her mother (oh she missed her) who gave them to her, and she loved little Jonah and Lola and Emmitt and she still loved John . . . a little.

Lucy felt better. Her life, her happiness, was after all not the business of anyone else or any circumstance. It was her business! It was all up to her and it was all so simple, so clear now. She would love again!

She felt a beam of sunlit energy and for the first time ever in her life, she knew what had to be . . . what she had to be. She would be in charge of the rest of her days! She felt the warm spring sun on her shoulders and realized how much she loved that feeling. She was that bean sprout, slowly poking her head out of the ground. She knew, if she were going to love again, things were going to have to change. If she was going to look for and embrace the things she loved, she was also going to rid herself of what she did not love. She would never be shy about things again. This was her life to live, and it would be done on her terms.

Sensing some change in their mother, the kids stopped crying as she got up from the garden, went into the kitchen, and got a jug of vinegar. She went straight to the tool shed and poured the vinegar into John's batch of fermenting mash. She did not love what drink did to her husband, and if she were going to keep loving him, there were going to be some changes.

Through the next ten children, through the wars, the depression, the tenant houses, John's death, and her broken hip, Lucy knew what she loved and what she did not, and she was not shy about it.

Back at the dinner table, I knew I had seriously overplayed my hand. After ninety-two years of life experience, Grandma Lucy had tried to pass a kernel of truth to me, and I had lectured her on what I'd picked up in little more than a decade.

I had no cards left to play. I shoved a big spoonful of beans into my mouth . . . and that made it worse. The beans melted into me. They brought sensations that I didn't know existed but now felt familiar, like they had always been in my mouth. They were a part of me.

I retreated to my internal dialogue, my innate reviewing and questioning process. *Why was I so short with Grandma?* The answer came in a moment.

I had stopped taking her seriously when she began having the visions. While I watched morning cartoons, she would tell me of her nightly conversations with people long departed. She named them all and told me of their features, their warnings, and their positions floating around her room. I had never before been close to the process of separation from this life. I did not know it was common for those about to depart this world to start having contact with the next. I just thought she was losing her mind.

Not long after that disastrous dinner, on my birthday to be exact, Grandma Lucy passed at the age of ninety-two, the second August passing of a grandmother but the first I saw up close. It would not be nearly the last in that house. I came to think of the dog days of August as a time when Sand Ridge watermelons ripened, I had birthdays, and grannies died next door.

My teenage years were occupied with other grandmothers, sports, school, BB guns, bicycles, motorcycles, hunting, and fishing. My waking hours and my dreams were full, and Lucy's memory took its place on the dusty shelves of my mind.

I breezed through my parents' high school and left home to find myself and get an education. My flirtations and indulgences were many, but when I finally brought myself into focus in the big, often-foggy mirror of life, I saw a path-with-a-heart, spirit-seeking, Woodstock-era flower child looking back at me . . . with an engineering degree and a penchant for world travel and adventure.

My search for a spiritual path took me across the "Crack in the Cosmic Egg," and into a "Separate Reality." I hitchhiked around Europe, ran with the bulls, and tried to drink all the wine in southern France before finally giving in to the economic pressures that beset many middle-class students. I got a job.

I was always in search of a path with heart. I meditated, did yoga, turned off my internal dialogue, and hugged as many trees in as many places as I could. I was still a seeker of spirits.

Years passed, and one day, from a friend of a friend, a fellow seeker, I got the phone number of a local psychic who said she might be willing to give me a reading. I was given specific instructions as to what I should say to gain an audience. I was nervous and surprised when, after a short phone conversation, the psychic politely asked me to come to her house.

I arrived early, still nervous as I entered her home. We sat at her dining room table and chatted, and after a short pause she tilted her head and stared out the window. Finally, when she came back to me, she said, "Did you realize you have a guardian angel?"

Intrigued, but a little skeptical, I asked, "Is that like a Spirit Guide?"

The old seer closed her eyes, and after a long silence she said, "You were her blue baby."

Now her eyes were open, looking through me. In a quiet voice she asked, "Do you know Lucille"?

It took a moment for it to sink in as the memories came flowing back. "Yes," I said. "Lucy, my mother's grandmother."

"Well, Miss Lucy has been with you for years."

I was too stunned to speak. My internal dialogue searched for an explanation. *How does she know my great-grandmother's name?*

"Beans," she added after a pause.

"What?"

"Yes, beans," she said. "She's been watching over you for years, protecting you, because . . . she wants to make sure you eat your beans, and that you've figured out how to love."

Turtles

Grandmothers were not that impressed, but BB guns and bicycles were what I was best at. Since Uncle Dick, the patriarch of the family, didn't visit the front porch of Granny's store with much regularity, I felt the need to show off as much as I could while he was there.

Uncle Dick and my surrogate grandfathers, the old men who congregated on the porch, were conducting daily business while seated on the sturdy, surplus construction-site bench from the "atomic plant" built a decade before.

Facing out onto the road leading to the Ohio River, the four-posted porch sheltered the full length of storefront, including the bench, two gas pumps, an air hose, a kerosene pump, a used oilcan barrel, and a vintage Fairbanks-Morse scale.

Mr. Willie, Humpy, and Uncle Dick were on the bench beneath one of the big four-pane windows looking out at the road. Calmo was facing them, squatting on the short concrete base of the No-nox gas pump. I listened to the mostly old stories of past hardships, droughts, floods, and how badly the young tobacco plants needed a rain.

As Calmo started an often-heard story, I got up and went

through the double Bunny Bread screen doors to the cold-drink box just inside. Pulling upwards, I expertly uncoupled the used cap reservoir from beneath the bottle opener and emptied the contents into the nearby trash box so that I could better pick out those that had survived the opening process with the least damage.

Back out through the screen doors, I marched with purpose along the length of the bench and off the porch, into the gravel parking lot under the shadow of the big, pole-mounted Gulf Oil sign. I raked in loose red gravel to better stand the slightly bent bottle caps on their edges facing the porch before pacing long steps back to a position directly front and center of the assembled crowd.

There was a brief pause in the conversation as I turned, took aim, and sent a single copper BB crashing into each bottle cap as fast as I could re-cock my Daisy pump gun.

When I finished and looked over at the bench, Mr. Willie was the only one who seemed to be paying any attention.

"That's pretty good shooting, Robert," he said.

Uncle Dick didn't seem to notice anything worthy of comment. He drained his Pepsi and continued discussing how high the 1937 flood waters had gotten.

The Pepsi gave me an idea. I took the empty bottle out amongst the dead bottle tops and carefully positioned it on its side in the gravel, its flat bottom pointed away and its narrow mouth inclined up toward the porch. I again took my center-stage position and summoned the spirit of Annie Oakley.

Again, Mr. Willie was the only one providing commentary. "Your Granny won't like you bustin' that bottle," he said as I fired.

The spherical projectile passed cleanly though the distant small opening, down the length of the bottle, and knocked out its bottom. Mr. Willie smiled and shook his head, but Uncle Dick still didn't acknowledge my amazing achievement.

Undeterred, I considered my other tricks. I could show him the bicycle cavalry! I took four empty metal oil cans from the trash barrel and set two on either side of the tarred-rock road in front of the store. I retrieved my Schwinn from its home in the garage out back and came roaring across the parking lot, steering with one hand and holding my weapon in the other. Fifty yards up the road toward Raymond's pond I turned around and surveyed my task. Building up speed slowly, the speedometer pressing toward fifteen miles per hour as I stopped pedaling, I let go of both handlebars and started shooting and re-cocking, *plink*, *plunk*, *plink*, *plunk*, as all BB's found their targets.

When I rode my bike triumphantly onto the concrete of the porch, Uncle Dick was staring out across the field, reviewing the chances of Bob Gibson and the St. Louis Cardinals making it to the World Series.

Out of ideas and disappointed, I put the kickstand down on my bike and quietly took a low seat on the old platform scales at the end of the porch, looking for my next opportunity. A fat sparrow started his glide down from the top of the triangular Royal Crown sign at the edge of Mrs. Pippin's tobacco patch; instinctively, I swung the gun up to my shoulder and in mid-air the sparrow crumpled to the ground, a rumpled pile of feathers!

Finally, Uncle Dick was looking at the dead sparrow. After a long blank stare across time, he asked, "Carry that thing with you everywhere, don't you?"

"I guess I do," was my honest reply, glad to have his attention at last.

"They didn't have BB guns when I was a boy. I used to carry

a little .22 that my brother, your granddad, gave me. I'd shoot anything that moved."

There was another long pause. "I remember we were cutting hay one year, and I was having a big time shooting rabbits out in the hay field. I must have killed ten or twelve as they broke cover to get away from that sickle-bar mower. I was driving the wagonload up to the barn, all proud of myself, when this big ole swamp rabbit hopped up out of the ditch onto the shoulder of the road just ahead of me and stood on its hind legs, looking at me.

"I tightened the reins to stop the team and that rabbit still stood there, as calm as could be, staring at me. He didn't flinch as I reached under the seat and pulled out my rifle. It stood there looking right at me as I shot him between the eyes."

Uncle Dick paused and looked down.

"I got ashamed of myself. I didn't need to do that, I had plenty of meat. I took it home and gave it to the dogs and felt pretty bad about it; him just setting there looking at me. I can still see him plain as day setting there on the side of the road just looking at me. I've dreamed about that rabbit so often that now I don't know whether it really happened or whether it was all a dream, I'm just not sure . . . but I don't shoot much anymore."

The porch was quiet. I didn't understand and didn't know how to respond. Finally, Humpy broke the silence with a discussion of the best hunting dogs of past and present.

I was done with showing off. I had other business anyway. Crocket and I were supposed to go fishing at Raymond's pond that afternoon and I wanted to get there early with my BB gun. If the fish weren't biting I could amuse myself shooting whatever expendable or dangerous target presented itself, including grasshoppers, starlings, dragonflies, frogs, snakes, and turtles. The latter three were particularly coveted targets, especially snakes, because they were snakes and were dangerous and there was considerable newsworthiness in killing one, especially if it was a cottonmouth or a copperhead. All the snakes I killed were assuredly of those varieties. The world was a safer place because of me and my BB gun.

Frogs were plentiful and provided good sport. They would stick their noses out of the water near the bank to breathe at short, unpredictable intervals. You had to be quick and accurate like with a bird or grasshopper on the wing.

Snakes and frogs had a one-time usage. If hit, frogs could be depended on to float or to be knocked up on the bank by a shot; snakes were usually found in shallow water, where their final fate could be easily verified. But turtles were a tougher, more durable target because a single hit was seldom fatal. A big snapping turtle had to stick his breathing snorkel, on the tip of his nose, up above the water to get a breath of fresh air every so often. My practiced and watchful eye was trained to spot and exploit this necessity by quickly launching a BB across the pond. The sound of the projectile as it struck told whether a hit had been scored; a sharp *whap* with little splash defined a direct hit, while a duller *thunk* and a spray of water said the BB had hit the pond first.

Whole mornings could be spent playing this game. It was like an epic sea battle between a submarine and a destroyer—waiting, watching, speculating where the periscope would appear next. The prey was good at utilizing the natural cover of weeds along the bank and appearing first on one side of the pond, then in a completely different area the next time. It was a real contest of strategy between a turtle and an eleven year old. These recyclable targets provided hours of diversion.

Uncle Dick's story about the rabbit had only struck a minor

chord in me, but I had little regard for lesser beings and none at all for snakes or turtles. They were the enemy who lurked in the grass and on the slimy, dark bottoms of ponds. Their big ugly heads, yellow eyes, and menacing mouths made it easy to regard turtles as villains. There were stories of snapping turtles biting off fingers and . . . other appendages; these were disturbing stories of caution to boys about skinny dipping where snapping turtles were around.

Local wisdom said that snapping turtles held on till they heard thunder, and would even hold on to people's body parts after their heads were cut off. Occasionally a big snapping turtle would interrupt fishing by clamping down on a hook, breaking or straightening it, and stealing the worm. These were enough signs of hostile intention for me not to feel guilty about my relentless harassment of turtles. I didn't feel any worse about turtles than I did about the worms I was impaling to fish with.

With my BB gun, tackle box, and fishing pole, I walked the hundred yards up the road to the pond, leaving my tackle and pole at the gate while quietly stalking the pond, hoping to catch unsuspecting critters by surprise. Sure enough, I quickly picked out a small, fist-sized head sticking high out of the water near the far bank. *Whap!* the BB struck green flesh.

I was elated. That was as solid a hit as I'd ever had, and you could tell by the way water and mud had roiled up that I'd done some real damage.

After a minute or so, with the alarm having been broadcast that a hunter was on the prowl, there were no more immediate targets. I retrieved my gear and got back to the business of fishing. I set the cork to the proper depth, impaled a worm on the hook, and guided it out to a likely spot in the pond before settling back to a comfortable position under the shade of the big sycamore.

I turned to the sound of water dripping and looked to the left edge of the pond. I saw what appeared to be two large, mud-green shells, armored land tanks, crawling out of the water onto the pond bank. I'd never seen that before! *Is this an attack?* I thought.

I shifted my body around and leveled my gun across my knees. I didn't have a good shot at their heads yet, and the BBs bounced off the thick shells. I waited. Now, clear of the water, leaving a red, bloody trail, the turtles slowly followed the curve of the bank toward me, finally giving me a glimpse of oozing head gashes and accusing eyes. I could see their faces now, scarred and bleeding, their eyes yellow and menacing. It was a sickening sight. I wanted to throw up. I wanted them to stop! I fired directly into the grotesque faces now coming straight for me. The bullets were on target but did nothing but open another hideous wound! Panicking, I fired again and again, bursting eyeballs, splatting sprays of red and yellow fluid misery onto the green grass canvas. Still they came toward me, larger and more grotesque with each labored push from those short, ghastly legs.

Can nothing stop them or put them and me out of this grisly misery?

Then I heard them. They had voices! They began talking to me, asking me again and again, "Why? Why?" I didn't have an answer. I didn't know! I just wanted them to die to be out of their misery. I didn't want to see their suffering. I wanted them to stop and go away. *Why couldn't they just have floated like the frogs?* I kept shooting, but every shot made their suffering and mine worse. I wanted to run, but I was frozen in place, held till they got to me.

What are they going to do to me? Why did I start this stupid game anyway? Please, don't come any closer! NO! NO!

Something grabbed me, shook me.

"Robert! Robert, what's wrong?"

I looked up to see Crocket standing over me with eyes wide. "You can't catch fish while your sleeping," he said. My heart felt like it would break through my ribs. I didn't answer, but looked back toward my attackers. They were gone.

"I guess I was dreaming, but man, it seemed real," I said as I scanned the bank and gasped loudly.

"What in the world is that?" he said, pointing toward the red bloody trail going around the pond bank and disappearing at the water's edge.

"I don't know," I lied.

Sometimes I still see those faces in my dreams. I don't shoot much anymore.

Fox

I've never been one to let modesty stand in the way of the truth.

I was explaining to my older buddies out on the front porch of Granny's store just how good I was at working in tobacco. I was sure there wasn't anybody in McCracken or Ballard Counties who could approach my speed at cutting or spiking. I couldn't tell if they were paying much attention to me or not. All three of them had their heads down, carving lazily with their pocket knives on the exposed area of the wooden bench between their legs.

Finally, Humpy turned his shaggy old head up toward me and said, "I know it's hard for a young'un like you to believe, but they's people what knows a lot more 'bout terbacky than you. People's been ah growing it down here fer more than a hunnerd years, back fore they had all this fancy equipment and chemicals that does most of the work fer 'em. Now they got spray dope that kills the suckers, the weeds, and the worms. They got gas fer gettin' the beds ready in the spring and machines that put the plants in the ground fer ya, and cultivators an tractors so's you hardly have ta use a hoe. Back in our day, we's out there in the patch when the sun come up and didn't leave till it went down, settin' and choppin' and suckerin'. Yes sir, there's plenty you don't know 'bout raisin a crop of leaf. And as far as speed is concerned, there ain't a one of these old boys on this here porch what couldn't a give you a run fer your money."

He paused a moment in reflection.

"Fox might still tan your hide. Him and your granddaddy was always the fastest around and he's the only one of us left that ain't all crippled up with the roomatiz."

Holding up a hand with stiff curled fingers, he went on. "Look at this old hand, son. It looks more like a claw than a hand! You'll know how it feels someday, son. When the younguns can't understand and you can't show'um anymore, when you been doin' somethin' all your life and then some young whippersnapper's been doing it fer a couple of years is the world's expert . . . you'll understand then!"

He went back to adding to the pile of bench shavings building up between his feet. He was right in one respect: it was hard for me to believe they could have done it any better back then, but I could tell he was stirred up and I didn't want to argue with him.

It wasn't more than a day or two later that Fox showed up on the front porch. He wasn't a daily front porch regular, but it wasn't unusual for him to show up every now and then to pick up a gallon of milk, a loaf of bread, or a carton of drinks and pass the afternoon with the fellas.

They were talking about so-and-so's daughter, and who she married, and which one of her boys got killed in the war, and how high the water got in the '37 flood, and an ornery old mule Emmett Warford used to own.

After considerable recollection about the names of the Ohio River steamboats that they used to stack wood for down at Ogden, Joppa, and Carrico Landings, Fox turned to look me in the eye and said in his high, nasal twang, "I understand your pretty good at puttin' up t'backer, son? It don't surprise me none. You're built just like your grandpa."

This was not the first time I'd heard the comparison, but it sounded different coming from Fox. I made no answer. My dad's dad had departed this realm long before I came into it.

After a pause, he said, "Ya wanna help me house my crop this year? Pay ya a dollar and a half an hour an o'course the wife'll feed ya dinner. What's ya say? We'll start in the mornin'?"

"Sure, Fox, I'll help you."

"Fine. See ya at the house tomorrow 'bout time the dew gets off."

Draining the last of his Coca-Cola, he sat the bottle under the bench, winked at Humpy, and got up. I watched as his old pickup truck left the gravel lot and rounded the curve by Raymond's pond.

I was excited, not because I liked to cut tobacco that much, but about getting to work with Fox, a local legend. Cutting tobacco was about the dirtiest, nastiest, most back-breaking job a West Kentucky farmer had to accomplish. Bent over all day, swinging a big hatchet would blister your hand, wear out your best arm, and permanently rearrange your vertebrae. The big, damp leaves were always in your face stinging your eyes, and the hand not blistered by the knife would accumulate a layer of sticky tobacco gum from guiding the thick stalks into piles. At the end of the day, one hand will be bandaged and the other will have to be drenched in ammonia, kerosene, or something stronger to cut the gum off.

From the stories I'd heard all my life, I knew Fox and my granddad had been best buddies. At eighty years old, Fox was still the unquestioned gold standard of tobacco field performers. I was going to get the chance to work with him in his own field, to gauge myself against the legend.

I had learned early on that there's something special about shared hardship. Putting yourself in someone else's field, working together under the same sun, doing the same things, strips away all the differences in age and experience and lets you get to know a person more than is possible by any amount of conversation. I was anxious to know who Fox really was, what he knew, what made him tick, and now I was getting my chance.

The next morning, I was out in the field at his place well before the dew was off, surveying the crop from the end of his patch. I shouldn't have been, but I was surprised: he had as fine a crop of Burley tobacco as I'd ever seen. It stood well over six feet tall. At the ground the stalks were as big around as the business end of a baseball bat, and the yellowing bottom leaves were uniformly more than a foot and a half across.

Fox came out of the house a few minutes later, walked up to me, and after a pause said, "Well, I reckon we might as well get started."

Unlike what they do up in Central Kentucky, where they cut and spike on the same pass down the field, down in Western Kentucky they'd go through the patch cutting the plants and placing them in piles of four or five to let the big leaves wilt a bit before beginning the spiking process. Kids too young to handle the knives and big stalks would "drop sticks," coming behind the cutters and placing four-foot-long hickory or oak sticks beside each pile. Weather permitting, Fox preferred the old tradition of cutting his entire patch and letting it wilt overnight before he started spiking the plants onto the wooden sticks. He felt it reduced waste from leaf breakage and gave him a better finished product.

As the rest of the crew was arriving, knives in hand, Fox and I walked over to the outside rows. It was his patch and the lead man sets the pace for everyone else, so I waited for him to start cutting the first two rows. As he began, I watched in amazement. He was not using the standard cutting and piling process I was familiar with. He was doing it completely differently than anything I'd ever seen before. He was going down the field backwards, leading with his butt!

Backing up between the first two rows of tall plants, he bent and twisted to his right, reaching across his body with his left hand to grab the plant stem about halfway up. Swinging his homemade hatchet underneath that arm with a downward backhand stroke to his right, he would cleanly sever the big stalk in one smooth stroke, laying the plant gently to rest on the ground. Without straightening up, or any other wasted motion, he'd pivot and swing the blade back across his body to the left, effortlessly cutting through a stalk in the other row before guiding it softly to the pile with his free hand.

Back and forth in this smooth ballet, he was taking long, even steps backward down the row. Mesmerized by the dance and the fluid motion of his old body, I watched him cut ten or more plants before I got started. When I finally did begin, I could tell that my forward-facing method, highly regarded till now, was crude and awkward in comparison, involving much more wasted motion and with the tobacco leaves continually in my face, stinging my eyes.

I worked as fast as I could, faster than I'd ever gone before, and still he widened his lead on me, finishing about seven piles ahead. At the end of the field I looked back at the rest of the crew. They were only halfway through their rows! Fox was twice as fast as these experienced cutters.

I was wringing wet as we walked back down to the beginning of the patch to the water jug. Fox's shirt was dry; he'd hardly broken a sweat.

I've never been one to hold on to a bad idea just because a better one wasn't mine, and I figured that I had better learn this backward cutting method quickly or this old man was going to kill me today. After the drink, I waited as Fox got started on the next two rows. I went over the motions in my head before I put them in action. *Right, left, right.* When I finally started, my forehand stroke across my body to the left was fine, but my backhand stroke to the right was pitiful. I could not cut the plant in a single swing; my hatchet always got stuck halfway into the woody stalk, forcing me to waste time and energy to pry it out, always splintering the stem badly with two or more weak and imprecise hacks before the plant came free.

I couldn't get enough power or the right angle or something on my back stroke, and I was falling farther and farther behind Fox.

Far behind and frustrated, I looked up and saw Fox had stopped and was looking back at me, smiling.

"You picked that up pretty good, son, cept you're swinging off the wrong foot! When you come back across to the right, swing off your left foot. Then just before your blade hits, give your wrist a little twist, like this," he illustrated.

"Thanks, I'll try it." It was amazing that just a small adjustment could make such a big difference; everything was much easier now, just a little shift in weight and a subtle twist of the wrist at the right moment and I was sailing down those rows with Fox. Fox and I cut two rows to everybody else's one that day. We got more than an acre and a half cut.

Granny was closing when I got back to the store. Mom had kept supper on the table for me. I laid my aching body gingerly into bed.

At first I thought I was dreaming, that it was some sort of

cruel joke my mind was playing on me when suddenly, after barely blinking, it was morning again and I had to get up and go back to Fox's tobacco patch. My muscles had recovered somewhat, but my bones had not.

I dragged myself out of bed with the thought that today was going to be my day to surprise old Fox. He'd surprised me with that backward cutting thing, but today I had a trick up my sleeve. I intended to use granddad's tobacco spike that my dad had given me. No bigger round than a half-dollar at its base, it sloped up gently into a smooth and perfect cone with a sharp point. It was not at all like those new store-bought spikes, which were short and stumpy with a large oval opening that could accommodate even the widest of the new-sawn sticks but would often split a stalk all the way out to the end. You could tell my spike was made out of good steel. When you'd used it a little and got the rust knocked off, it had a deep blue shine and it pinged like a tuning fork when the stalk popped over it and onto the stick. It was my turn to surprise Fox.

That morning, I was out in Fox's patch early and started spiking without waiting for anyone else. The younger boys had followed behind the cutting yesterday and dropped an old split hickory stick or a newer sawed oak one beside each pile. I picked up the first stick, stuck the bigger end in the ground, and placed my special spike on the top at the other end. I grabbed the first plant on the pile near its cut end and hefted it up, keeping it parallel to the ground, and brought its stem to rest momentarily on the sharp end of the spike, the tip about a foot or so up from my hand. With a quick snap of the wrist I pushed down, making the spike split through the stem, threading the plant down onto the stick. The spike pinged loudly as it popped through the stalk. I bent over, pushing the stalk all the way to the bottom of the stick, leaving room for the others. Without standing up, I took the next plant from the pile and in one motion lifted it to the tip of the spike before repeating the process.

When the five stalks in the pile were threaded and spaced evenly on the stick, I removed the spike, sidestepped to the next pile, and began again. I was the one flowing down the row now, and just beginning to get my rhythm when I heard something coming from the row behind me, a steady *ping, ping, ping.* Wheeling around, I saw Fox. He had a spike just like mine!

"Where'd you get that spike, Fox?" I demanded, surprised and a little irritated.

He paused a second then smiled and said, "You know, me and your granddad grew up together." Pointing down the road, he said, "He lived right over there at the old home place. We was best buddies. He might as well have been my brother, as much as we played, worked, hunted, and fished together. We could perteneer put words in each other's mouths. When we got old enough to work t'bakker, not just drop sticks, we went down to Uncle Lute Smith's place there on the corner and he made us a couple of spikes just alike, outa an old harrow blade. Let's see, that would'a been in nineteen aught five I guess. That there spike of yourn, ain't it got five notches filed in the bottom there?"

I looked at my spike and along the bottom edge there were five V-shaped notches.

So much for my surprise, I groused.

He looked like he was about to say something else, but stopped and went back to work. We spiked out the rest of that row and started walking back to the end of the field to begin another pass, when he said, "Like I said the other day, you're built a lot like your granddad. With your shirt off and me behind you coming up that row, it seemed like fifty years ago and me and him coming up that old row with them spikes singing like we did many a time." He started to say something else, but then got a strange sad look on his face and looked down as we walked back to the water jug at the edge of the field.

When I finished my drink, Fox was looking at me like he had something on his mind. Finally, he said, "I'm gonna tell you something, son."

"OK, Fox. What?"

"You know what hurts an old fella more than anything?"

"What's that, Fox?"

"Things that ain't got no reason, things that's done and gone and can't be brought back. Not just things you've done, but what others done. Things like . . . like that first big war, son. There weren't no sense at all in them boys having to go over there and get kilt." He paused and with moistening eyes went on. ". . . and there weren't no reason for that polecat shooting your grandpa either. I was with him when they got in an argument over that mule. It didn't amount to a hill of beans and then that rascal laid over there in them woods and waited for us to come up that road, and he shot your grandpa dead, right out there in that road, with me setting right beside him. Him with a wife, and leaving them three kids without a paw. I never felt so sorry for a widow and kids in all my life. I tried to help them get along as much as I could. I give them boys work when they got big enough. They all turned out good to have no paw like that, but there just weren't no reason for it, it just didn't make no sense!"

Spent, he dropped his head, turned, and went over to the next row and started spiking.

After a moment I went over and started down the row behind him. I had never heard that story. I knew my father's dad had died young, but I had never heard what happened. I was in a daze, in another world, another time. A dam had burst, and time came gushing down that old row, washing over me. I floated with it down the field. Things shifted, like I was washed across a line and was suddenly old, like I had been out there in this same field, under this same sun, with this same person, doing this same job since time began. We were moving, but time was not. Our spirits floated down that old, familiar field, just the two of us, together again, until all the rows of piles had been spiked except the last two. Fox and I started them sadly. All the rest of the crew was at the barn or loading the tobacco-laden sticks onto wagons and taking them there.

Neither one of us was paying much attention to where we were or how much was left of this crop, this day, or this experience, till I heard some loud yelling coming from the end of the field. I looked up and saw the old fellas from Granny's front porch. They had driven out and were sitting on an empty wagon at the end of the field.

"Look at ole Fox. I told you he could still whip the best of you young colts," Humpy shouted.

I hadn't been paying any attention, but now looking up, I saw Fox was indeed three or four piles ahead of me about halfway down the row. I instinctively started picking up the pace. Everything else being equal, I was a lot younger and had a little more wind than Fox did. Soon I pulled even with him and finally edged past him a little. I could hear him breathing harder and harder. I was at least a pile and a half ahead of him with less than five piles to go.

The crowd was now silent. Everyone could see I was going to beat him. I was going to beat the legend, and they knew it! They were going to talk about this on Granny's porch for years to come. I was going to be the new legend, the one they used as the standard for all the younger boys. I couldn't lose. I picked up the next stalk and set it up on the point of the spike ready to shove it down when that flood rushed back inside my head. Without thinking, I put my knee against the old stick. As I shoved the stalk down, I pushed sideways on the stick till the wood snapped.

"Broke stick," I yelled, as I grabbed another from the pile ahead and one of the young boys ran over with a replacement. By the time I got the spiked stalks off the broken stick and on to the new one, Fox was almost a full pile ahead. I put on a fast and furious finish, but he finished his row at least half a pile ahead of me.

You would have thought that it was the Fourth of July and those old fellas were twenty years younger, the way they jumped off that wagon bed and ran over to us. They were laughing and yelling and patting Fox on the back and telling me how they had "told me so," and maybe I'd get better next year.

"Ain't gonna raise no crop next year," Fox interrupted, wiping sweat from his head with a bandana handkerchief. "My grandson has been after me to let him have this allotment. I may help him a bit, but it'll be his crop."

The old fellas loaded back into the pickup and headed back to the front porch, eager to tell the story, as Fox and I walked back down that dusty old row for the last time, back to get our gear, back to the water jug and our own ages.

I uncorked the spigot and lifted the jug high over my head to get a long drink. As I held it there I heard him ask, "Why did you do that, son? I saw what you did. Why didn't you go ahead and beat me? You could've."

I had every intention of denying what the old man was talking about until I lowered the jug and looked into those sharp, clear eyes staring out from that worn, wrinkled old face. I could sense that he "perteneer" knew what words would come out of my mouth. I said them anyway.

"Fox, there just weren't no reason for it, it just didn't make no sense, buddy."

Hal & George

Every day I'd watch George walk the quarter mile between his house and the grocery, and every day he'd pause in the same spot and stare off into the fields for a moment, talking to someone. Curious, I walked down the road toward the river and paused at a dark spot in the pavement. I hadn't noticed it before. Later, I started asking questions about it on the porch when George wasn't around. Here's the story I was able to put together.

Hal and George were brothers. Both left Western Kentucky in their teens. Hal went to Henry Ford's Detroit to work in the car factories, and George went to the muddy, bloody trenches of France to save Europe. It changed them both. Hal came back to the river bottoms and fields of home to apply mass production, industrial logistics, and machinery to the farm. George learned about the mass destruction of industrial slaughter and came home trying to forget everything machinery could do. They lived across the road from each other. George, the eldest son, on the home place, and Hal just across the gravel road in a farm he bought with Detroit savings.

Full of energy and new ideas, Hal soon turned his farm into a finely tuned agricultural plant with well-tended fields, a stock barn full of hay, a corn crib full of yellow corn, a fine bull to service his herd of Herefords, a prized Rhode Island Red rooster, a good wife, and a dozen kids to share the work.

George, much to Hal's disgust, didn't seem to have any plans except to sit on the front porch swing and stare out across Hal's well-ordered fields, fences, and ponds. He sat out there in every season, except in the worst of winter days and in the fall, when the sound of hunters' guns drove him to the basement. He didn't take much interest in farming. He could live well enough on some disabled veteran's benefit and his share of the tobacco allotment that came with the home place that he let Hal raise on the halves.

George was permanently invited for Sunday dinner at Hal's, and in shade tree conversations afterward, Hal occasionally asked about the war. George usually didn't have much to say, but Hal persisted until one Sunday, in response to a question about how it felt to be a decorated and wounded veteran, a thoughtful George said, "Just a minute." He got up and went across the road to his house and returned with an Army service jacket.

"Here," he said handing it to Hal. "It's yours."

George had not counted on and was not comfortable with all the questions Hal and the kids had about the old uniform, but he answered most of them.

"What's that," asked Hal's oldest boy, Billy, pointing at a gold, metallic-thread, V-shaped insignia on the right sleeve.

"A Wound Chevron," answered George.

"You got wounded?" Junior asked excitedly.

George nodded.

"How'd you get it?" asked Hal.

"You don't want to know," said George, shaking his head.

"You can turn this in and get one of those new Purple Heart medals. You know?"

George shrugged. "I got more reminders than I need," he said as he got up and went back across the road to his basement.

Weeks later, after Sunday dinner, Hal, beaming with pride, made a big deal of presenting George with a box. "Look what the government sent you," he said.

Inside lay a Purple Heart. George looked up at Hal. "Thanks, but you keep it. I gave you the uniform, you can keep this too."

"But we're proud of you," said Hal.

"I know."

Trying to hide his disappointment, Hal thought a minute before carefully pinning the medal inside the chest pocket of his Duck Head bib overalls, over his heart but hidden from sight.

"It's an honor. Thank you," Hal said. "Is it OK if I wear it this way?"

George nodded.

Occasionally, at Hal's urging, they would walk the old farm and George would listen quietly, nodding his head as Hal made suggestions—what should be planted in this or that field, how he should mow this pasture and cut those horse weeds, repair this barn and find a good woman, start a family and get his life back on track. Of course, he could always let Hal manage the farm and split the costs and profits. George eventually came to be amenable to the latter idea, but with some stipulations, including a ban on hunting and shooting on the property.

With enthusiasm, Hal started a detailed assessment of the vacant fields and buildings, developing a plan to bring it back to life. Things went well until he arrived at the old stock barn; to his horror, he saw large, baseball-sized rat holes permeating the dry, hard-packed floor. Everywhere, scores of them! Obviously, a whole squatters' colony of the destructive vermin had built a labyrinth of burrows and tunnels under the barn.

Hal, thinking of his corn crib full of freshly harvested yellow corn just across the road, was more than a little aggravated. This was intolerable! *How could George let this happen to the home place?*

Confronted as to why he had not taken steps to eradicate the pestilence, George shrugged. Trying to say something that Hal could understand, all he could come up with was said softly under his breath: "I've seen enough killing for a lifetime, Hal. Killing has its price."

Hal fumed and argued till they worked up a compromise. If Hal wanted to do something, George agreed. "Fine, but it's all on you. Just as long as it don't involve explosions or shooting or me; and you gotta clean the place up, like it never happened, so I don't have to see it."

Hal promised. He went back home and started planning, coming up with idea after idea on ways to rid George's farm of the pestilence while meeting George's stipulations. After much thought, he came up with the simplest plan of all. He'd inform some of the local boys of the rules, offer a generous reward, and leave the details to them. He made the offer to his sons and any local boy who was interested: a five-cent bounty for every rat carcass brought to him in a tow sack. Billy and a buddy were enthusiastic about the deal and got to work immediately.

It was not as easy as the boys thought. They had little immediate success stalking the barn with clubs and chopping hoes, and soon lost interest in the task. Instead, they explored other rundown buildings and sheds on the farm.

To their delight, they discovered an old Model T truck, thick with dust, in an outbuilding. Forgetting about the bounty, they turned their attention to the truck. A little oil and gasoline and a few turns on the crank brought the old relic sputtering to life. The thick blue smoke rolling out of the tail pipe soon sent them coughing and hacking out into the fresh air, but it gave them an idea, putting them back on track with their primary purpose.

Huffing and puffing, they pushed and pulled the old machine over to the stock barn. They fitted one end of a flexible hose tightly over the truck's exhaust pipe and stuck the other end into one of the many tunnel entrances. After tamping dirt in around the hose they began stuffing rags, tow sacks, horse blankets, and dirt into every other entrance they could find, leaving only a few selected escape routes open.

Delighted at reports of the plan, Hal chose not to inform George, fearing a prohibition on the use of poison gas, not currently banned in the agreement. Instead, Hal watched from his porch. The boys, armed with clubs and hoes, cranked the Model T and took up positions.

They had no idea what they had stumbled on. A few inches under their feet was a sprawling underground metropolis, painstakingly excavated, complete with warehouses, dining facilities, public areas, playgrounds, condominiums, post offices, nurseries, and shopping malls. Every rat that ranged within five square miles either lived, worked, shopped, or came to socialize in the complex.

Hearing the sound of the old vehicle, Hal moved out to the edge of his yard, watching intently from across the road. What happened next has been the subject of much conversation over the years. At first there was no activity at all. Then, as if on signal from rat sergeants blowing whistles, secret gates were flung open and a solid wave of squealing, brown-furred, tail-dragging vermin went out over the top, surging from their underground warrens over the scarred bare dirt of no man's land in front of the barn. The verminous horde completely obscured the ground and sent the startled boys into a screaming, weapons-dropping full retreat in front of the massive charge.

This was not a helter-skelter, pell-mell charge, but a well-scouted and organized rat charge into the fescue and toward the road, marching directly at their primary objective: Hal's corn crib.

Seeing the boys running and yelling, Hal moved toward the action. He ran down the road, stopping in its middle to get a better view just as the leading edge of angry, screeching fur flowed under the fence, filled the ditch, and spilled out over the road. This was not a pack of ten or a hundred; this was a thundering herd, a legion of thousands, more than any man could, or should, ever face.

Though surprised and caught off guard, Hal stood his ground, stomping and kicking furiously into the surging wave. He grabbed his overall legs and hiked them up to his knees, shaking out the nasty things that were already climbing and biting their way up his pant legs, trying to stem the tide, hell-bent on his corn crib! Known for uttering very few cuss words, Hal strung together whole verses and chapters of profanity as he defended his property.

From a distance you might have laughed, thinking that he had suddenly succumbed to his Celtic roots and lapsed into an impromptu Irish river dancer as he pumped his knees up and down in grim, furious choreography. Slick with rat blood and offal squirting out from under his farm boots, the road was becoming a dangerous place for dancing! In an instant, Hal went down with a blood-curdling scream that penetrated his brother's scarred eardrums . . . and brought flashbacks.

George came running out of the house too late. The scream

and Hal were both gone before George had jumped off the porch, buckling his bad leg and falling to the ground. The sea of furry, razor-mouthed piranha was in a full-gore feeding frenzy, biting and tearing at Hal's clothes, feasting on the sensitive soft parts first—eyeballs, tongue, and . . . elsewhere—stripping flesh from bone before being pushed away by later ravenous waves. When George hobbled close enough to see, there wasn't much left; a dark, sticky circle on the road, a few patches of blood-soaked overalls, a few metal pocket snaps, Hal's pocket watch, and the Purple Heart, lodged between bare, wet ribs, facing where the heart had been.

George stood over the remains. He'd seen worse, lots worse. The memories came flooding back as he stood above his brother in the road. He slowly bent down and picked up the gory medal, holding it for a moment before returning it to Hal's chest, facing out now.

"I wasn't supposed to see this again Hal," he said bitterly. "I told you! You didn't want to know!"

Tommy

It was past lunch and they had been gone all morning. Tommy and I hadn't been able to eat, play catch, go fishing, or do any of our normal things; we could talk or think about nothing else.

Our frustratingly clandestine fathers had left early in Dad's pickup, hopefully to return with every thirteen-year-old boy's dream: motorcycles. We really didn't care whether they came from Europe, Japan, or the US; as long as they had two wheels and a motor, we would make do.

The day and the watching dragged intolerably on, like a long-winded preacher. Mercifully, in the middle of the afternoon the truck came into view . . . and . . . *YES!* A tarpaulin was stretched over something in the truck bed.

Like excited puppies, we ran alongside the truck as it pulled into the gravel lot of Granny's grocery store. We caught glimpses of red and sparkling chrome from under the edges of the tarp. Before they could stop the truck, we were scrambling up to untie the ropes, pulling the covering aside to reveal beauty beyond imagination—black leather seats, chrome mufflers, cream and red gas tanks, red and chrome shock absorbers, red fenders, and *Yes! Yes!* the Harley-Davidson logo right there on the tanks! *Wow!*

We swarmed over the truck bed drunk with excitement, trying to soak up all the glorious mechanical details: the perfectly proportioned, single-piston, 50 cc two-cycle, air-cooled motors, with a three-speed shifter on the left handlebar grips.

Our dads were smiling broadly, enjoying our excitement.

Our moms came out of the house, worried but enjoying our glee.

It seemed forever till we got them unloaded and carefully lifted to the ground. We inspected every detail: kick starters, kickstands, gas throttles, clutch levers, front brakes, back brakes, fuel cutoffs, carburetors!

At long last, astride the beasts, we checked out the speedometers, light controls, horns, and fuel levels. When absolutely necessary, we studied the manuals for the correct fuel mixture.

The motorcycles were identical, only one number difference in the serial numbers. The question now was which of us got which bike, but that wasn't really a problem.

Tommy and I, both August-born only children, were like brothers; if our parents would have permitted it, we would have moved in together. We were an inseparable team. We both carried 1950 half-dollars and had long ago developed a system for settling childhood disputes, for deciding who got to go first, for sharing, and for avoiding hard feelings. With no prompting, Tommy reached into his pocket and pulled out his half-dollar, flipping it in the air, letting it land in the driveway. We didn't have to call it—heads was his and tales was mine.

Heads! There were never any hard feelings, but Tommy always seemed to win the big ones . . . though going first was not always a blessing.

The bikes were the same and I really didn't care which one I got. Tommy hesitated only a moment before jumping on the one nearest.

"Let's start it up," Tommy said to his dad.

Our fathers did their best to remember the instructions from the dealer, showing us the basics, the essential details. There was so much to remember, just like *Sky King*'s preflight checklist. Switch on, gas on, in neutral, throttle advanced, kick starter out and foot positioned. Finally, a good kick and the oily blue smoke rolled out the exhaust as the little motor sputtered to life. *Vroom, Vroom.* Smiling, Tommy revved the motor with a twist of the right grip, testing, learning.

I was next. One kick on the starter and it sounded like two angry bumblebees. Sitting on that bike, still on the center kickstand, I had seldom been happier in my thirteen years on earth.

We were both accomplished bicycle riders and had grown up driving tractors, but neither of us had any experience with the physical dexterity necessary to coordinate a controlled release of the left-hand clutch lever while increasing the engine speed with a right-hand throttle twist while keeping the thing upright and straight as it jerked into forward motion . . . and that was just the beginning! Simultaneously you then built up speed, pulled in on the clutch, let off on the gas, rotated the shifter, increased the gas, and let out the clutch again. The soft grass of our back yard was a good choice. The air was torn with the sounds of over-revved motors and grinding gears.

Our moms started to wonder anew whether this was such a good idea. Our dads were beginning to wonder if the gears, clutches, and blue jeans would last through this learning process.

Gradually we got better, to the point that each of us could shift through all three gears in the length of the back yard and not run into a tree or through a flower bed. We were ready for the parking lot, and then the country road in front of the grocery.

What a different and exciting world, a magic summer. Hills that had meant long minutes of standing up hard on bicycle pedals were now ascended with the slightest twist of the wrist. The world speeding by and the wind pulling at your face was a slice of heaven. It was a world we never knew existed, a world we were now a part of. I looked over at Tommy beside me, eyes squinted against the wind, and marveled at how we were going forty miles an hour and yet seemed to be frozen in space relative to each other—the genesis of my understanding of physics.

That summer felt like the beginning of life; freed from the encumbrances of time and distance, the world shrank for us. No longer did it take half an hour to get to Crawford Lake or over to the swimming hole on Matlock Lane. It was now a fun five minutes.

Suddenly, we were at the top of the preteen motorbike pecking order, the envy of our friends, many of whom had the less expensive and slightly slower two-speed Sears mopeds. We were in the big time with real Harley-Davidsons. No matter that they were made in Italy, they had the Harley-Davidson name right on the gas tank.

Tommy and I became even more inseparable. Every moment of every day we were exploring speed, ourselves, our machines, and the world. We rode side by side or single file, weaving back and forth to miss the white lines down the centers of the narrow country roads. We pulled wheelies and leaned into corners—a particularly strange and pleasing maneuver. We were amazed at how far we could lean the machines over—so far over that rubber was scraped off the bottoms of the foot pegs.

We started to see and feel the geometry and physics of it. Riding side by side on straightaways was much easier than keeping in formation around corners. Going around corners side by side was tricky, if not downright dangerous, requiring precise choreography of speed, position, brakes, bike, and body.

The inside track around a corner is always shorter, so the outside bike must speed up or the inside bike slow down to maintain positioning. Navigating the narrow, no-room-for-error boundary between our bikes, the sand and rock–strewn road edge, the ditch, and the barbed wire fence beyond, we learned precise, near-telepathic communication and trust in ourselves and in each other.

We went well beyond simply holding formation around corners. We developed what we called the "butterfly crisscross," switching positions in mid-curve! When the inside bike's rear taillight was only barely ahead of the trailing bike's front tire, we swapped positions. It had to be precise. A fraction of an inch from a life-threatening event, its edgy grace changed us.

The summer had its minor mishaps, and by the end of July both we and our bikes were well-seasoned road veterans, each with distinguishing dings and scratches.

Our birth month was busy and hot. When Tommy got a break from working on his family's farm and I wasn't hauling hay, you could find our motorcycles at our headquarters: the Newton Creek Bridge on Matlock Lane, where we were likely to be splashing around in one of the several deep pools just upstream. The steep creek bank, with its overhanging trees and high-hanging grapevines, was a Tarzan wannabe's heaven. We tried to reproduce the distinctive yell ("AUUUUGH!") on the downswing and let go at the perfect moment to splash into the deepest part of the cool water.

One bright Saturday afternoon, Tommy and I came across a promising new vine anchored in multiple locations high in the sycamores along the creek. Any new vine, mutually discovered and hacked free, had to have a first test flight and pilot; the pilot decision was left to the half-dollars.

Tails. I got to go first. We cut the vine with a hatchet and I tested it with my weight a few times before leaping off the high bank. It was a solid flight until, just before I let go of the vine, it let go of its anchors; instead of landing in the water, I landed on the hard, gravelly creek bank. My knee, up under my chin, slammed my jaw together hard enough to chip a tooth. Sometimes winning the coin toss wasn't so lucky.

I wasn't into swimming anymore, so we dressed and went back to our bikes for a ride around country back roads before heading back down Matlock Lane. Practiced veterans of this road, we were side by side coming down the hill and into the S-curves. I was on the inside. We danced through the left turn with the butterfly maneuver ever so gracefully, as we had done a hundred times before. I saw a grin on Tommy's face as we pulled even with each other on the short straightaway before the next curve. Our timing had never been better. I was in the middle of the road now, coming up to the right-hand curve. Braking, leaning, judging, we reversed again as I pulled to the outside track and Tommy again took the middle of the road.

It felt so good, so powerful, to be in touch with someone's mind and movement, to be a team. I saw him nod and knew he meant to fly the bridge. We built up speed for the little ramp where the asphalt road met the settling old wooden bridge. Launching from this mismatched elevation, we flew halfway across the bridge and roared up the hill side by side.

At the top of the hill, our lives changed forever. As if from another dimension, a truck suddenly popped into our world, and time slowed. On the outside, next to the ditch, I had a narrow pathway through, but not Tommy.

In the corner of my mind's eye, I saw the flash. First, Tommy's motorcycle was at my left shoulder and then in an instant was behind me; stuck in the front grill of the truck. Tommy, launched up from his seat, was still beside me, flying in slow motion, up over the hood. Our eyes locked and massive amounts of data, full of questions, flowed between us. His widened eyes were filled with those questions. *What's happening? Is this IT?*

His upper torso cleared the cab, but his knee caught the windshield's upper edge and started him tumbling in a slow somersault out over the truck bed, our eyes still locked, asking questions we had never asked before, questions for which neither of us knew the answers.

For long seconds we traveled side by side, me earthbound, him flying, until his head splashed onto the pavement. I saw a flash of light.

I stomped on the rear brake, leaned, and twisted the handlebars left as I let the bike slide away from me down the road and stepped clear, back up the road toward Tommy.

I reached him as the dark pool grew behind his head. I looked into his eyes, but he was not there. I knew the road would always bear the stain, no matter how many times it was repaved. I'd seen it before.

I remember little of the next few days. It was my first pallbearing job and my first out-of-body experience. At the church, I was outside my body, floating around, witnessing the other, guilty part of me. *It could have so easily been me! Why wasn't it me? Is Tommy mad?*

The magic summer was over. Other summers came and went,

but none found me turning down Matlock Lane to the bridge or the dark spot beyond. Legend often sprouts from untimely deaths, and in the years that followed the accident there were stories of strange occurrences at the old bridge. I knew what was there, and it took me a long time to confront it.

It took monumental trust, and not a small number of promises, for my parents to allow me to keep riding motorcycles through the rest of high school. It was a small community, and reports reaching my parents did nothing but reinforce my responsible diligence. A week before I left for college, I was rewarded with a new bike, a much bigger one. For me, it was the end of one journey and the beginning of another, one that I needed to share with Tommy.

On the day I was to leave for college, the day Tommy and I had talked about, the day that would change everything, I rode my new bike down to Matlock Lane.

The old bridge was familiar in every detail. I smiled, thinking that few people besides Tommy and I knew that the timbers had been ordered by my dad at the County Road Department and cut at David Gibbs's sawmill. It was the last publicly maintained wooden bridge in the county. I parked on the pavement, just off the bridge, and walked out onto it. I threw pebbles in the stream and remembered flying with Tommy. I said goodbye and asked his forgiveness for not being in his place.

In the far distance, I heard a motorcycle. Probably just my imagination. I held that belief until the sound became undeniable—a motorcycle was headed toward me.

I smiled at the thought of younger generations just beginning to enjoy their magic summers. I heard the change of gears as it slowed to turn onto the lane off Ingleside Road. Mentally, I tracked the sequence of events: the gear shifts, the strain of that slight hill before the decent into the creek valley, the acceleration down the hill toward the curves.

The sound grew louder as I looked through the trees to catch a glimpse of who was coming. I heard the rider slow and shift as he approached the first curve. It brought back memories. I heard the throttle open coming out of the curve, speeding up, shifting in the short straightaway. I would have to wait till that next curve to get a clear look at the rider. I was betting it was one of the Massa boys. The motor slowed. *I should be able to see it . . . just about . . . now!* I saw nothing. *What*? I reevaluated everything. Were my eyes and ears playing tricks on me? Was I hallucinating? Was death coming for me too?

The throttle opened as the bike came out of the curve. My ears knew the sound was in the right place, but my eyes saw nothing! A hundred yards away, on a straight road, it bore down on me. I braced myself. I heard the distinctly "tinny" motor wind tight before going into a higher gear; louder and louder it came till I couldn't tell the difference between my heart beat and the motor.

The bridge and I both shook and trembled as the bike hit the old timbers. And then it stopped, the motor idling a bit longer before . . . silence. It felt right in front of me, no more than a yard away. Old sensations came flooding back: the hot smell of the little two-stroke engine, the popping sounds of a cooling motor. My heart was racing faster than the motor had been. *Is it my turn to go?* I looked for those eyes.

"I miss you Tommy and I'm sorry it had to be you first! Maybe it should have been me?"

Waiting for an answer, I heard a metallic sound at my feet. I looked down . . . a 1950 half-dollar lay on the bridge timbers at my feet. Heads. He had to go first. No hard feelings.

Hitchhiker

Brylcreemed hair and a silvery tongue,
Slick had been a con man, since he was young.
"Let me sell you this Edsel with sixty thousand miles,
Two bucket seats and a dash full of dials."
"I can tell right now you look pretty thrifty,
Let me sell you this Ford for thirty-seven fifty!"
"Let me sell you this van, give you a real good deal
At two thousand dollars, it's a virtual steal."
He said the engine was new and the body, I could see,
He hated to let it go but he would for me.
I drove it home in a December snow,
And on Christmas Day named it, Vincent Van Go.
It looked real good and it ran just right
Till I drove it in the river on a Saturday night.
Got water in the carburetor, water in the crank,
In no time at all that Volkswagen sank.

I must have been living in a dream world because I felt no reason for concern. A friend who worked at a garage had flushed the muddy water out of Vincent's motor, and after all, it was a marvel of German engineering. What did I have to fear? What could possibly go wrong?

A week later, I headed out on my first of many cross-country adventures.

I took essential reading material: a copy of the *Whole Earth Catalog*, *The Electric Kool-Aid Acid Test*, and Jack Kerouac's *On the Road*. The engine sounded better with each inhale as I headed down the Western Kentucky Parkway.

I stopped briefly at my parents' home near Monkey's Eyebrow, where my dad gave me his assessment of my purchase. "Son, I don't like the engine being in the rear. I think you ought to bought something made over here."

At this point in my life, I was far beyond such advice. I was headed out to meet Gurney Norman's Divine Right Davenport in the Great Rocky Mountain highlands.

Growing up in the river bottom flatlands of Western Kentucky, I didn't know what a mountain over 3,000 foot looked like. I thought all mountain passes were like Cumberland Gap, and from the backseat of my family's Pontiac, Cumberland Gap had made little impression on me. Still, I expected this to be somewhat different—this was the Rockies!

At Dallas, I noticed Vincent didn't seem to have as much power as when I started. By the time we got to Denver, he was struggling with internal conflict. Finally, the ascent up to the 11,000-foot-high Monarch Pass over the Continental Divide ripped the heart out of him. Vincent threw a rod through the block, far worse than the mutilated ear of his namesake. Not to be deterred, I left the van at a garage in Gunnison and started hitchhiking. The lighthearted trip had taken a heavier turn into a bad-dream driveway.

All roads south of Gunnison, Colorado, are drawn downward, as if in a vortex, toward the San Juan Mountains and Red Mountain Pass. I'd read some of the construction history of the pass. Back in the '30s, when a dime would get you and a date into the movies, it cost a million dollars a mile and scores of lives to carve the twisted semblance of a road hanging off vertical cliffs through Red Mountain Pass. I had no idea what awaited me.

I was spiraling down toward Durango and the ancient city of Mesa Verde. In mid-afternoon, I stood outside Ouray, Colorado, at the northern mouth of the Red Monster. The sky was crystal blue, and the afternoon sun made the vertical mountainside bright crimson. The only smudge on the landscape was a thick column of smoke coming out of a gulch somewhere to the east.

I must have been lost in my thoughts and the beauty of the surroundings, because when I looked back up the road toward the pass, there sat an old green-and-white Dodge Window Van. It must have passed and pulled off on the shoulder without me noticing. An arm stuck out of the driver's-side window, waving me up toward it. *My people! Hippies!*

I hoisted my backpack and hurried up to the opened side doors.

"Thanks," I said as I threw in my belongings and climbed in the back.

"I'm headed to Durango. You going that far?" I asked.

Turning to greet me from behind the wheel was a tall, pale, young, Nordic-looking guy with sleepless red eyes, a thin smile, and long blond hair. He nodded without a word. In the front seat, with the engine cover separating them, I could see the edges of what appeared to be a young blonde with a child in her lap. She did not turn to acknowledge me. I figured she did not want to disturb the child. I pulled the doors closed behind me as the van started up the hill.

I could tell the van was an old Slant Six from the strain of the engine going uphill. I looked around. *A Window Van. Great. I bet the scenery will be awesome.*

When we got to the top, I had expected to see the road descending below us in a series of switchbacks, like my ride in the tow truck going down into Gunnison. Instead, as we topped the crest of the hill, the earth disappeared. I felt like I had been launched into outer space, weightless and floating.

I stood on my knees for a look out the front windshield to see the driver steering us down a tiny ribbon of asphalt that looked like it had been half chiseled into and half glued onto the side of the vertical cliff wall. From my perspective, it looked like the van's mirror was slicing through blood-colored rock. I couldn't imagine more than a sliver of the outside tire tread gripping the edge. There was no guardrail.

Flicking past in a blur, I tried to focus on some of the hundreds of memorial crosses spiked to the cliff wall along the twenty-five miles of goat-path, twisty-turny, no-guardrail terror. I suspected the red cliffs were stained dark with blood from the hundreds of memorialized victims. I knew the color of blood on asphalt.

Gripping the rear of the engine cowling, I steadied myself for a look to the left. I wished I hadn't. Thousands of feet below, I could see the patchy canopy of the pine forest. Then my heart came up in my throat as I looked out the front windshield and saw oncoming traffic. Quickly, I sat back down and braced for the crash. Instead of the bone-shattering impact I had expected, I heard only a *whoosh* as the other car, by some miracle, passed. Or maybe not, maybe at the last second in this deadly game of chicken he had veered off into the canyon below. I didn't want to look out any more.

Like whistling in the graveyard, I tried to make conversation as the van rocked from side to side.

"Narrow road isn't it?" No response. I tried again. "Beautiful day, isn't it? I wonder what all that smoke was from. Did you see it?"

That got a reaction! The girl in the front seat, without turning, said in a flat, cold voice, "Yes, we saw it too. I'm afraid it came from Genuine Johnson's house as it burned to the ground."

The van jerked violently to the right. I was going to die, I knew it. Head down, eyes closed, and breathing deeply, I sat cross-legged with my arms bracing against the violently careening green-metal coffin. I prayed for this to be over and that my cross would be pretty and my name spelled right.

I don't remember much after that. I either fell mercifully asleep or, more likely, I was toppled from my perch and knocked unconscious against the side of the van. The next thing I knew, I was lying with my head on my backpack in a park in Durango, well after dark. A check of my body and belongings revealed nothing missing except maybe a small piece of my sanity.

Confused, shaky, and hungry, I walked across the street to a conveniently located local restaurant, Panhandler Pies. I ordered dinner and sat trying to decide if it had all been a bad dream . . . and if it was still going on. I ordered a beer and the house special and tried to go over in my mind what had happened that day. My food came and I started paying more attention to the other customers, trying to decide if they were still part of the dream or not.

At the bar, I heard the bartender say, "Can I get you another one, Genuine?"

Genuine? I thought. *Could that be a coincidence?* After a long mental search of my extensive TV cowboy drama protocols, I decided to be very cautious about approaching what looked from the back like a "real" cowboy at a bar. I waited till a spot opened up beside him before I went over. He barely nodded as I sat down.

"Genuine . . . that's not a common name," I said, "and I've heard it twice today already."

After a long, silent moment, the grizzled old cowboy turned toward me and in a tired half snarl, responded, "Yeah, and what did you hear?"

I told him about seeing the smoke over in Ouray and that someone told me it was Genuine Johnson's place that had burned down. "I just wondered . . ."

The man's face grew ashen and his eyes dulled as the whole restaurant became oppressively quiet. Finally, letting out a long sigh, he said, "Much obliged, stranger. I'll take care of it." He and the bartender exchanged looks. Then he finished his beer, slowly got off the bar stool, and left.

I found a hotel room, but didn't sleep well; green vans and crosses flashed through my mind all night. The next morning, I went back to the restaurant for breakfast. The owner recognized me and, without speaking, came over and tossed a paper down in front of me. The headline read, "Local Man Dies in Crash on Anniversary of Tragic Wreck."

What?!

The story told how Genuine Johnson of Durango had apparently swerved off the road in Red Mountain Pass the night before. The story highlighted the coincidence of another crash exactly one year earlier, in which Mr. Johnson, driving under the influence, had collided with and killed a young family of three on the same stretch of road.

When I finished the story, I looked up and the owner was staring at me. "Genuine never drove that road at night anymore. He kept an apartment here in town. Said he had bad dreams!"

I nodded and after a while I asked, "Was it green?"

"What do you mean?" the owner asked.

"The family he killed . . . they were in a green-and-white Dodge Window Van, weren't they?"

The man's eyes grew wide. "How'd you know that?"

"I had a bad dream too," I said.

Buzz

It didn't surprise any of us to hear that Buzz was dead, or that he had been shot in the back in a bar in Colorado, but it did unexpectedly invoke a cryptically extracted promise made years before.

Buzz could, simultaneously and in nearly equal measure, evoke both love and hate for almost every acquaintance. There was a very short lag time between a thought entering his mind and the often prophetic but always unpolished gems emerging from his mouth. I knew of several instances in which his girlfriend, Rose, if she'd had quick access to a gun, might have saved him the trouble of traveling all the way to Colorado to get shot.

Once, at the late-night and gratefully mellow Simon-and-Garfunkel wind down of a raucous party, with only the oldest and closest friends remaining, Buzz tried to stir things up. After thoughtfully surveying the room, he abruptly and dramatically jumped up from the couch to announce, with heartfelt conviction, that he was "the biggest man in the room" . . . or at least that specific parts of him were bigger. All of us knew better than to take the Buzz bait—things could escalate quickly. His proclamation drew no immediate response.

Unacknowledged, Buzz continued, "Well, by God, it's true and I can prove it," he said, turning toward Rose.

"You used to live with Brent, and everybody knows about Larry and Bob. You've slept with all the boys here, so go ahead and tell 'em the truth, Rose!"

Rose's dark eyes shot bullets of black outrage from her rapidly purpling face.

Still meeting with only amused stares, Buzz gave up, sat down, and grew uncharacteristically quiet for a while. Looking around the room again and focusing on Rose for long seconds, he softened and apologized to her and to all of us. Waxing as eloquently as I'd ever heard, he acknowledged his crudeness and continued by saying that we were really all that he had, the only people in the world that came close to understanding him and loving him; we had always stood by him in spite of all his considerable and obvious foibles; it meant more to him than he had words to say, except that, he would always be there for us, and hoped we'd be there for him.

Looking around the room into each eye individually, Buzz raised his glass and asked, "Will you all be there?"

This was classic Buzz. None of us were sure what he had in mind, but it was not a moment he was going to let pass. Again he scanned each face, making sure each glass was raised as we all gave our pledge to, "be there for him," whatever that meant. If you were going to be around Buzz, you had to expect an unpolished gem from time to time.

Buzz was an unpredictable study in contrasts: a civil engineer working for the state, a part-time biker/drug dealer, a longhaired flower child, and a heavy contributor to the Boy Scouts of America and Big Brothers.

In the car on the way to the little Central Kentucky town

where Buzz had been born and where he was to be laid to rest, the four of us told stories of that night and reminisced about many others. We arrived early at the church, went inside, and walked up to the coffin before any other guests came in. It took some getting used to, but it was Buzz all right; the nose and the scar were unmistakable, but the hair was cut short and he was in a suit and tie. We'd never seen him like that, but realized it was his mother's prerogative to restore him to the son she had always hoped he would be. Other mourners started to file in, and the organist started playing traditional church hymns as we took our seats. Bob Dylan or the Grateful Dead would have been more appropriate, but his mother was in charge of Buzz's last rites.

Sitting in the back, we could pick out Buzz's resemblance to people sitting in the family section. Without incident, the preacher began the service. Except for the fact that he had never actually met Buzz, he was giving a solid rendition of Buzz's better works, most of which had occurred in high school. He was glossing over some of the later, seedier details of Buzz's life and starting to wrap up when we heard the first *BBLOOOM, BBLOOM* of a big motorcycle in the distance, maybe two of them. A tense murmur went up in the chapel. I glanced about at other faces and could sense a growing apprehension and restlessness. The sound grew louder, *BBBLLOOOOM, BBBLLOOOMM, BBBLLOOOMMM*, as it became evident that this was not a fluke. People looked around at each other with questioning and fear-filled eyes. The noise and apparent number of machines grew larger and louder as the preacher lost his concentration and began to stumble in his delivery. *BBBLLOOOOM, BBBLLOOOMM, BBBLLOOOMMM*, the church was abuzz with whispers as the din grew with every second. Any thought of this being a coincidence disappeared as the roaring horde turned into the church parking lot and circled the building like vultures. The rumbling shook the small sanctuary, and the people in it were talking in low, urgent tones, bumping around like molecules of water beginning to boil. There was real fear now, a feeling of being surrounded, as walls, flowers, and people all vibrated with the overpowering rumble.

Then, as if on cue, there came sudden silence . . . the deathly eerie silence before a storm. A loud bang on the side door broke the suffocating quiet and triggered a collective pew-shaking jump. The nervous pastor, looking to the family for guidance, got none. He bowed his head slightly, uttering a short, silent prayer before making the decision to leave the pulpit and go to the side door. Through the cracked door, I could see shiny black helmets and leather. After short negotiations, the door opened wide and they began to file in. Beer cans were concealed in Iron Crossed helmets and half pints were shoved into shiny rear pockets as they queued up to the coffin. There must have been sixty or more: men with long, greasy hair and bushy beards, girls in skintight jeans, all in black leathers emblazoned with *Harley* and winged skulls. As the first ones reached the coffin, we could hear muffled comments, like, "Shit, is that Buzz? What did they do to his hair, man?" They were a bit loud, but not unorderly. It took ten minutes for them to file past and make their exit. Buzz was in charge of the funeral now.

The visibly shaken pastor mopped his forehead with a white handkerchief, closed the door, and concluded the service with a few more generic lines.

The funeral procession was one the town would long remember. The hearse was followed by ten or so cars and then the bikers, two abreast, stretching from one side of town to the other. The unmuffled engines were deafening, and crowds of townspeople lined the streets to watch.

To the great relief of the family, at the cemetery the bikers broke away from the procession and left. The short graveside ceremony was uneventful and uninspiring, punctuated only by the usual sobbing, hugging, and tearful goodbyes. The crowd dispersed and left the gravediggers to do their job.

We went back to our car, but we didn't leave. With the mourners gone, we came back and watched as the cemetery workers went about the business of removing the fake grass covering the dirt pile, lowering the coffin, and dismantling the machinery of interment. We offered each of them five bucks and a beer to let us fill in the hole; they were more than happy to accommodate. Brent finished a beer and tossed the empty into the hole, Rose picked some daffodils and scattered them on the coffin. After several more layers of earth, we sprinkled some of his favorite herb seed on the loose dirt.

Holding hands, we stood silently in the fading light, sending our energies to the other side. As we left, Rose placed a rough piece of black obsidian on the mound, an unpolished gem brought back from the Colorado mountains.

Weeks later, Rose got a card from Buzz's mother. She thanked us and told us how much it meant to her, and to Buzz, for us "to be there for him."

The author, age ten, and all the grandmothers and great-grandmothers who lived next door or across the street. *Back row, left to right:* Mary Cecilia Ford (Lily Tomlin's grandmother), Myrtle Parker, Della Brigman, and Annie Brame. *Front row:* Lucy Starks and the author.

Sally Hodges Thompson, the only grandma to not spend her last days in Ragland.

Granny Parker on the porch of the family grocery, late 1940s.

Roy Parker, the author's grandfather, with an Ohio River catfish, about 1950.

The author with Granny Parker (far right) and two sisters, Evey (left) and Louva, on her one and only visit to the concrete pier where her husband drowned in Ohio River backwater.

Grandma Lucy York Starks and the author, age four, on a Sunday visit to Evey's at Grahamville.

Grandma Starks and the author, age eight, watching TV.

Sunday dinner at Granny's, with family visiting from Detroit.

The author's first fish, caught in Raymond Long's pond. The family grocery is visible in the background.

Sherman “Fox” Ford at a family reunion in Paducah’s Noble Park. Lily Mae Tomlin, Fox’s sister and the actress’s mother, is in the background standing beside Fox’s wife, Myrtle.

The author at age fourteen, loading tobacco with Bill Christian and Bunk Carneal.

The author at age thirteen (right) with Tommy.

The author steering Vincent van Go to the Left Coast.

The author somewhere on the side of the road in Colorado.

Vincent van Go. The upside-down emblem is a metaphor for the era.

The author at Homer's tomb on the Greek island of Ios.

The servants' quarters at the ancestral home of the Balfour family in Glenrothes, Scotland, the site of the author's supernatural encounter. The photo is unedited, and the original print shows what are referred to as "spirit orbs." (2010)

The other Bob—Bob Kehrer—beside a P51 model at Leiston Airfield, where his dad left for his last combat mission. (2011)

Ablain-Saint-Nazaire, also known as Notre Dame de Lorette, is the largest French military cemetery in the world. The ossuary pictured here is surrounded by the graves of forty thousand French soldiers from the first, second, and third battles of Artois.

The lantern tower at Notre Dame de Lorette is meant as a guide for "lost travelers." It contains the remains of nearly six thousand unidentified French soldiers from World War I.

The Canadian memorial at Vimy Ridge. The statue, known as *Canada Bereft* or *Mother Canada,* weeps for all Canadians lost in World War I.

The author looking out of a German machine gun bunker above Omaha Beach, Normandy.

A German bunker at Utah Beach, Normandy.

The American cemetery overlooking Omaha Beach, Normandy.

The old guys on the front porch, late 1960s. *Left to right:* Monroe "Bunk" Carneal, John D. McElya, Sam Wray, Willy Turner, Halbert "Humpy" Morehead, and unknown. The author hand-lettered the sign in the background reading, "Parker & Thompson General Merchandise."

Fat Tuesday

I sat on the bench at the playground watching the parking lot, waiting for my son and granddaughter. I heard it before I saw it: a beautifully restored, late-sixties, red BMW coupe pulled into an empty space. The driver, about my age, likely there to meet a grandchild, got out of the car and took a nearby bench. The sight and sound of the car brought cold chills and took me to a different place, a parallel universe.

It was a new year and my last college semester; I had no doubt that adventure and change would soon explode into my reality. I was apprehensive and not a little excited. Already, my rural early life had undergone rapid and multiple transformations, from A's-without-trying high school hotshot to slide-rule toting, Pershing Rifle–uniformed and beer-sotted frat boy at Murray State, to full, cannabis-blossomed, butterfly-shirted, longhaired hippie and engineering near-graduate at the University of Kentucky.

I had a loose vision of life after the cocoon of college, but I hoped to be swept away by spontaneous outbreaks of karmic opportunity. Besides, reality was a greatly overused, narrow, and pejorative concept. If space, time, and light could be bent, then multiple and simultaneous parallel universes existed—so what did reality have to stand on? How could anyone believe they were actually in control?

At a Sunday afternoon party at Keith's house, just such an outbreak occurred when someone noted that Carnival was winding up in New Orleans, and Mardi Gras ("Fat Tuesday") was just a day and a half and eight hundred miles away. After a moment's reflection, Keith, back in school after Vietnam (and the owner of a red 1969 BMW coupe) informed the group that he was going, and wondered aloud who would go with him.

ROADTRIP! More than were serious spoke up, but Keith was locked-and-loaded, Marine Corp serious. He could seat three more. "We can leave tomorrow and get there for Fat Tuesday. Who's in?"

As the reality of life's accumulated restrictions settled sadly into most at the party, a raging internal debate developed in my head: . . . *but that damn Fluid Dynamics class has the real possibility of keeping me from graduating this semester . . . but then, will I ever again stand at this convergence of youth, freedom, and a chauffeured BMW?*

Mardi Gras. The name echoed around in my head. This Roman pagan celebration of fertility, older than Christianity, had proved so immune to suppression that the Catholic Church finally had given in and appropriated it as their own. Embracing it, the pope had put it in the official church calendar, allowing for two weeks of whatever debauchery and carnal behavior one could come up with, on the condition that on the last night before Ash Wednesday, all the remaining meat, eggs, cheese, liquor, and libido had to be gone before midnight, and the forty days thereafter had to be dedicated solely to fasting and begging repentance for what you'd just done. Rightly, this last day of partying came to be known as Fat Tuesday, and I could be there!

My inner debate was far from finished, but the words were out of my mouth before I could catch them, "OK, I'll go with you!"

It was after noon on Monday before the luggage was loaded, the coolers filled, the organics stashed, and we headed out Richmond Road to South I-75. The five hours of daylight went well, with me glad to share the driving in the solid little car; but long road trips are always more fun in anticipation and beginning than in the dark, tired middle or the red-eyed, head-nodding last few hours.

In the dreary hours after midnight, we came into a new reality, a space between lands. For long minutes, we had been droning along into the void on a monotonous and coma-inducingly straight, flat, and featureless highway.

NO, wait! We're on a freaky long bridge over water!

The short concrete curb and aluminum railings barely came up to the bottom of the car's window. The barrier did not impede our view into the cold black reality of death waiting in the water, neither did it seem likely to keep us safe from it. We were in a box with wheels racing along a ribbon laid on top of an ocean! I expected any moment to see Rod Serling or Jesus appear in the roadway, or Atlantis to rise beside us.

At sixty miles an hour, it took more than half an hour of dash-gripping, staring-through-the-windshield-into-eternity excitement to get across the twenty-four miles of the Pontchartrain Causeway. Had we known how many lives were lost building it or how many coffins on wheels had flown over that railing, we would have been more terrified.

The adrenalin had barely subsided when, at three in the morning, we were driving down Canal Street to the point where it ends at the Mississippi River. Our arrival was not heralded, and it struck us that beyond this moment we had no plans. We were winging it.

Spent and stupid from our eight-hundred-mile trip, our immediate choice was either a left or a right. We turned left into a gravel parking lot beside the railroad tracks, the last remaining vacancy of prime New Orleans real estate. Luckily, the guard shack was deserted. We drove around the barrier and went in to scout the lot. Its only feature was a fenced-off electric transformer station near one side. Keith, experienced in camouflage and clandestine operations in other worlds, pulled the car up close to the chain-link fence, opposite the guard shack, and we pitched our backpacker's tent on a patch of grass next to it.

Far too early, the dawn came grey, wet, and dripping into our tent. Rain from above, and Pink Floyd and Jimi Hendrix from somewhere, woke us up. Peeking out the zippered front door to see where the music was coming from, we spied another vehicle that had somehow snuck into the lot while we slept. It was an old, blue Ford Econoline van, with its two hinged side doors swung straight out, held open at the top by the balanced placement of an old and very wet mattress, making a perfect front porch for watching it rain. Focusing better, we could see three apparitions staring at us from chairs on the porch, waving for us to come on over.

With little debate, we cloaked ourselves in Army surplus ponchos and hurried over to their world. A fine and parallel world it was. We were soon best friends with the two guys from New York and the hitchhiker from Boston they'd picked up along the way. They were well supplied and generous with their breakfast—Budweiser and roll-your-own smokes. When it rains, it's often best to settle back and just let it rain.

We spent most of the morning enjoying the reality of a rainy day in the van's smoky interior, listening to 8-tracks, trading stories, and absorbing the amazing correspondence between rain-splashed puddles and *Dark Side of the Moon* and "Nights in White Satin."

We saw the parking lot attendant come on duty at the guard shack, a shadowy figure, his face hidden in a bright rain hood. We figured it was just a matter of time till a slack in the rain would bring him over to explain the parking lot rules and fees . . . and ask us to leave. We were not surprised when, during a lull in the monsoon, he came hurriedly toward us in his purple poncho. As he neared, we could tell he was our age. He stopped just outside the porch, studying us for a serious moment, respecting our boundary, before smiling and saying, "It's Fat Tuesday! Let's party dudes!"

The ice broken, we lit one up for him. In our toking and joking, Jules told us it was his last day on the job and "none of it matters anyway," because the parking lot was soon to be a huge aquarium.

"Screw it," he declared. "Tonight, the lot belongs to the people of Mardi Gras! Come on up to the shack in about an hour. I have some refreshments and we'll celebrate my last day at work," he said as he started back to his one-man sentry post.

The sun began to peek through the clouds, which gave hope for a clear, dry culmination of Mardi Gras.

After a trip back to the car to freshen up and change into party clothes, we straggled into the small group crowded around the entrance shack. Inside the shack, a big worksite water dispenser left room enough for two people, if they stood close.

My mouth felt full of cotton. I quickly located the paper cups and helped myself to several glasses of the cold strawberry Kool-Aid.

Jules, the host, standing just outside the door, looked at me with a wide grin.

"What's wrong, bro?" I said, as he handed me a cold bottle of beer.

"Nothing's wrong with me, but something's gonna be wrong with you! I noticed you hitting that electric Kool-Aid pretty heavy."

"Electric Kool-Aid!" I tried to be outwardly cool as panic struck my bowels.

"Yeah, I dissolved about a thousand micrograms of strawberry acid in that two gallons of Kool-Aid. Happy Mardi Gras!"

Outwardly, all I could say was, "OK. Thanks." Inwardly I had a lot of panicky things to say! *How long have I got? What's going to happen when this stuff really kicks in? What am I gonna do? Where am I going?*

I'd taken acid before, but in lesser amounts and always in more familiar confines. I was far from home at this cut-loose, throw-down, party-till-you-drop, let-the-good-times-roll, ground zero of total abandonment. The laws and realities of space, time, and light were already under severe strain here.

Alone, I walked up Canal Street, where I saw several monstrous floats rolling straight at me, gaining speed. Just before the parade consumed me it turned abruptly left onto Bourbon Street. I was pulled along in the backwash, floating down into the heart of the Vieux Carre into my new alien reality.

A thundering herd of Great Plains Buffalo, bellowing and snorting, had formed directly in front of me, making the earth quake. I stood upright and trembling, bracing for the transition into the next life, waiting to be trampled beneath the ten thousand hooves bearing down on me from every point on the compass. I clinched my teeth and shut my eyes, waiting, waiting for the tunnel of white light. It was delayed. I peered out to see what the hold-up was. I was on a tiny island enclosed in a sacred bubble that was splitting the monolithic herd only inches in front of me. I vibrated with the massive blur of energy flowing on every side. I chanced a step forward—the bubble followed.

Cool, it's a movable bubble!

The bubble went where I willed. I could take it with me. I began to move down the street, suddenly full of people again, but colors and faces blurred together until I could move no more. Something was wrong with my vehicle body. The motor was running, it was in gear, but the left side could gain neither traction nor permission to move. The right side tried rocking back and forth, but we were stuck.

This seemed the right place for a "pan left" camera movement, where a large fuzzy Keystone Kops gold badge, slightly off-center in a sea of blue, came into my Technicolor vision. The camera view tilted upward to a large, jowly cartoon face whose mouth was moving, emitting a low guttural, "Broooo, Broooo, Braaah, Brooo!"

Somewhere, part of my consciousness went into hyper mode. *A cop is holding my left arm.* The panic spread, communication circuits were overloaded! *Concentrate on what he's saying! Oh crap, I can't. He's going to lock me up, throw me in jail! Who can I get to bail me out?*

Another part of me was assessing the color of the vibes flowing between us and I wasn't getting much red, just gold, green, and purple, the official colors of Carnival. That settled me down a bit as I kept looking at the mouth, desperately trying to figure out what it was trying to tell me. I noticed a blue arm, with a swollen fleshy hand at the end of it, pointing at something ahead. I looked. The hand was pointing toward a trashcan.

Ding, Ding, Ding! Bells went off in my head. *I am still carrying the beer bottle, and glass containers of any type are not allowed on the street. I knew that! He wants me to put it in the trash can!*

It all made perfect sense now, and as I focused on moving toward the receptacle, my left side was suddenly free. The adventure continued.

The universe was moving so fast that people from other dimensions were revealing themselves. Buddha, Moses, Don Genaro, and Lupercus, with his goat-skinned priests, were all celebrating with me.

I was starting to get used to this. I could function in this . . . maybe. I nodded at a hammer-headed shark creature with one eye and tried to find a place to sit down out of the main flow. I needed time to assimilate. I found an unoccupied doorstep, sat down, and contemplated my fate. After all, this was not really new ground—Captain Kirk had been trapped in a Tholian Web during a period of spatial interphase.

I tried to think what outcomes were likely. The largest question looming was, *Will I ever come down from this trip? Maybe not . . . so if I don't . . .will this be my reality . . . for the rest of my life?*

It was not a comforting thought, but at least it was a solid thought in this otherwise fluid world. It was something I could build on. *Does objective reality really exist? Maybe reality exists only in my head and all that matters is how I deal with it!*

I started trying to get accustomed to the specters and frog-headed, antlered creatures cruising by. *If this is going to be my reality, I might as well get used to it.*

I was adjusting pretty well when Keith's face appeared, superimposed on a red balloon, inches from my face. I was glad he found me, but he was obviously not adjusting to this new world as well as I. He had that manic, don't-try-to-slow-me-down look.

Breathing heavily, expanding and contracting, he blurted, "Where have you been? Did you drink that Kool-Aid? We've got to go . . . I'm going. I'm outta here. This is too weird. Let's go!"

I had no problem with leaving. In my new reality, I was resigned to go with the flow.

Somehow, we found the BMW and were soon in full retreat, hurtling back across the black, cold water. The engine and Keith were wound tight; I could feel and see the vibrations. Going faster than our headlights, he strained through the windshield, making small, quick adjustments to the wheel with deadly seriousness.

Without warning, a red-lighted ballet was projected onto the windshield, into our reality.

A quarter mile ahead, a tanker trailer in our lane was side by side on the narrow bridge with another big semi-trailer truck. The tanker had locked its brakes and was beginning a classic pre-jackknife slide. The semi swerved left into the guardrail, sending sparks and rubber chunks flying back at us, pulling us into the dance! The semi careened right off the guardrail and slammed into the tanker. More sparks flew from the bumping and grinding behemoths. *Is this the birth or the death of something?* I liked the idea of fireworks to mark my passing from this reality to the next.

Closing too fast, we had no choice but to barge onstage with the two other characters. We swerved around debris as we went into a faster slide, catching up and nearly merging with the melee. Time slowed, every nanosecond vibrant and meaningful. Dancing to death's hot metal scream, we slid down center stage, every instant closer to that wrenching, sparking, steel wall blocking the rest of our lives.

Escape seemed improbable. I braced for the impact . . . but again I had to wait. In the blink of an eye, in the briefest of moments, a portal opened, a pathway between the grim dancers opened up and we shot the gap like the starship *Enterprise* squirting through a wormhole, a clear road ahead of us. I jerked around to see the hole quickly close and a huge fireball erupt as the tanker twisted sideways and exploded, the flash seared into my memory and the rearview mirror.

We sat in reflective silence as Keith drove straight through to Lexington. Neither of us ever again spoke a word about it.

My son and granddaughter pulled into the lot and my dream state was broken. I looked over to the stranger. He was gone, and so was the car. *Was I dreaming?*

The incident rekindled long-forgotten memories and made me go back and re-examine those days. In the intervening forty years, I had lost all track of Keith. Despite all efforts, I could not find a trace of him; it was as if he had never existed.

I searched through all my memorabilia, looking for some tangible proof of the events. All I came up with were a few photographs of porta potties in Jackson Square and an aluminum doubloon from the Endymion Krewe bearing the slogan "Token of Youth."

With the aid of the Internet I uncovered all sorts of interesting details about the 1973 Mardi Gras. I found the complete parade schedule, the weather report, and the fact that it was the last year floats were allowed in the French Quarter.

I perused old issues of the local newspapers, almost afraid of what I'd find. I had almost given up when . . . there it was, my story. In a March 7 newspaper, on the first day of Lent, the headline read: "2 Dead, 2 Injured in Fiery Causeway Crash."

Lucky Guy

In bright morning light, I was standing on the heel of Italy's boot, in the train station at Brindisi, trying to focus on the big wall map. I'd just gotten off the overnight ferry, tired but exhilarated after my water passage from Athens, and I was trying to plan the next part of my route to Pamplona, Spain.

I had wandered around Europe for the better part of three months, always going farther and farther east. Now I had mixed emotions about going, both geographically and emotionally, back west, toward home.

I was sad because I knew this was going to be the last and maybe the most exciting chapter in the story of my carefree youth. Once back, I knew I had to start the business of the rest of my life, not the least of which was to get a job and pay off my college loan. Within the next decade, I'd surely be married and maybe have a kid or two. I knew it would be a long time, if ever, before I'd be free to wander the globe as free as I was now.

I tried not to think of it. I still had the possibility of a great adventure in the next few days, a final, adrenaline-pumping experience that would either slingshot me back into a mundane world, pumped up with energy and excitement . . . or kill me! In four days, I was going to run with the bulls in the Fiesta San Fermin, just like Ernest Hemingway in the 1920s and the young vagabonds of my generation in *The Drifters*, James Michener's latest book.

I stepped to one side to see around the girl standing between me and the railway map on the outside wall of the station. Immediately, as if our minds were linked, she placed her finger on the map and started tracing a rail line up the east coast of Italy to Florence, the exact route I was contemplating!

"Stop there," I mentally commanded as her finger suddenly halted at a rail junction. She started east toward Venice. "No, No," I shouted in my mind, and sure enough, the finger stopped, came back to Florence, and started north again to Milan.

WOW. My heart was beating faster now as she traced a path up through the Alps to Geneva. Was I suddenly clairvoyant? Had I acquired some cosmic power from that wordless windswept mountain day shared with a shepherd on the Greek island of Ios, or was she a reconnected long-lost part of me?

Whatever. I couldn't believe my fortune as her finger started south, down through Grenoble and into Southern France. I was more and more excited as she went along the French side of the Pyrenees and into Spain at the coastal town of Irun. As she traced the rail line back along the Spanish side of the mountains to Pamplona, it was hard to hold still from the vibrations shaking me from head to toe.

As men will do, I took one more inventory of her backside, steadied myself, and in my best and friendliest bass voice said, "Are you gonna run with the bulls?"

She turned to face me and in her eyes I saw myself.

"Yes."

This was a reconnection. We had been friends through several lifetimes. I was a lucky guy. The last chapter of my trip would not be maudlin and sad. I had an old ally to share the journey with.

We introduced ourselves and exchanged "where ya froms." She was Carol from Texas. Yes, she had read *The Drifters* and *The Sun Also Rises*, but she thought Hemingway was a "man's writer" without much empathy for his female characters.

The next train north didn't leave till early afternoon, so we checked our backpacks in lockers at the station and went into town for an early lunch. By the end of our meal we had agreed to travel together as far as Milan. There she would decide if she wanted to go alone east to Venice or to Pamplona with me.

On the train, through the evening and night, we shared our deepest fears and secrets. We were of the same spirit, long-lost allies that show up when you need them. She had a boyfriend back in Maine, and I had a girlfriend waiting in New York, and we both had fears that this trip would have profound effects on those relationships.

In the morning, in Milan, our connection held solid. She decided to stay with me at least to Geneva. In the beautiful Swiss capital we found a campground overlooking Lake Geneva and its four-hundred-foot fountain. We talked, toasted the Fourth of July with good Italian sparkling wine, and fell asleep in each other's arms under a bright canopy of stars.

The next morning we caught the train south, stopping at Grenoble to take the cable car up to the old fortress and have lunch. That's when we started talking about our feelings about religion, life, death, and bullfighting. Neither of us could put our finger on why we had been fascinated by Hemingway's and Michener's accounts of the Fiesta and bullfights, or why anyone would choose the profession of facing death.

We bought more wine, fruit, bread, and cheese in Grenoble and found a private and empty compartment on the train that would take us to Spain by morning. That evening, as we sped south and west out of the mountains and into Provence, we dove deeply into the wine, our fears, and our mortality.

I contended that life is all a matter of cosmic timing. It was timing that brought us together in Brindisi, it was timing that we had read the same books with the same effect, and if we made it to Pamplona for the Fiesta, it would then be time for . . . other decisions.

She offered that some things were serendipitous, but we choose to put ourselves in situations where things are more likely to happen. She reminded me that it was no fluke, it had been a conscious decision that we were going to be in Pamplona on the first day of the festival. If we were to die, it could not be written off as bad timing, like being struck by lightning or something.

I countered that when each of our time comes, it will come whether we're trying to be safe or not. I noted that, at the moment, we felt safe in our little compartment, but we were actually thousands of miles from home, speeding through strange mountains in a steel box driven by someone we didn't know, had never seen, and could not even communicate with. I said we might go to sleep tonight and never wake up again. All we really had was this moment and each other. With that note I kissed her, and we passed out with our arms around each other.

During the night, our train stopped in Lourdes, France, a small town north of the Pyrenees. Maybe I should have known a little more about the history along our route, especially since there is a Lourdes Hospital in my hometown of Paducah, Kentucky, but I was clueless. Catholics reading this will probably know that in the

1850s a fourteen-year-old girl named Bernadette claimed to have seen the Virgin Mary eighteen times in a grotto in Lourdes. Now this little town, about the size of Danville or Murray, Kentucky, has more hotel rooms than any town in France except for Paris. It is one of the world's great pilgrimage sites, with millions of visitors every year.

We slept soundly and didn't know that in the middle of the night, the entire train, including our previously private eight-person compartment, had been hijacked by a whole cloister of Dominican nuns.

Sometime the next morning, squinting out through half-opened eyes, my retinas were pierced by the blindingly white habits of no less than six frowning faces in the previously empty compartment, with dozens more visible out in the corridor. For a moment I panicked.

OH, MY GOD, I thought. *I'm dead. I've died and the Baptist Church hasn't prepared me for this. Catholics ARE in charge of who gets into heaven!*

My arm still behind Carol's back, I nudged her awake. She gasped at the sight.

As the initial shock died away, I was able to focus on other possibilities. *Maybe this isn't a judgment panel. Maybe we're all in this afterlife together, waiting to see where we're going. Maybe Brother Rogers had been right about Catholics—and me—and this was a gathering spot for the whole bunch of us going to Hell!*

I can't be sure if all this dialogue happened in my mind, if Carol and I were telepathically whispering, or if I had become so mentally transparent that the nuns could read my mind. All I know is that one frowning nun pointedly glanced at our ringless fingers, then at the empty wine bottles on the floor, and finally directed her gaze into my eyes. After a contemptuous pause, she said, "Young man, in the unlikely event that you and I should ever meet again, in this life or after, there will be no doubt that divine providence has been disproportionately lenient with you."

It took me awhile to decipher the precise words, to separate the sting from the acknowledgement. I was happy to realize I wasn't dead and I was also gratified to hear her acknowledge that I was a lucky guy.

To our great relief, the whole congregation departed within an hour or so, and by four o'clock that afternoon we were in the midst of one of the world's great parties, the Fiesta San Fermin. We found a place by the river where we could hide our packs and sleeping bags beneath some shrubs, and headed into town. It was a European Mardi Gras on steroids. We were caught up in the endless parades marching down ancient streets shouting, singing, and drinking wine from leather bladders. I never made it back to our sleeping bags, and as quickly as Carol came into my life, she was gone again. It did not disturb me. We were allies. I knew we would find each other again when we needed to, in some lifetime.

Before the sun came up the next morning, with no small quantity of Vino Tinto coursing through my veins, I stood atop the wooden street barriers that city workers had erected to channel the bulls from holding pens outside the city to the arena in the center of town. I was still unsure if I was prepared to face death that morning, or any morning.

In the distance, I heard trumpets and drums, and around the corner came another parade. This one was soberer, more somber, and full of costumed pageantry. I had stumbled onto the Parade of St. Fermi, the patron saint of Pamplona. I was transfixed by the spectacle until I spotted her, behind the priests at the head of the parade: the nun from the train! I was only a little surprised as her head snapped toward me, instantly picking me out in the crowd. Something was definitely going on with my connections! As our eyes met, and with her words echoing in my head, I knew she was also my ally.

Later that morning, from nearly the same spot that I saw her, I jumped into the street and ran in front of the bulls, protected by her advice and admonition, "Young man, in the unlikely event that you and I should ever meet again, in this life or after, there will be no doubt that divine providence has been disproportionately lenient with you."

She knew me, and she knew what I already suspected: I'm a very lucky guy.

Drumbeats

In the witching hours of Sunday morning, I lay in a sleepless bed in a strange, empty room and listened as the storm came with pounding waves of howling wind, driving rain, and rumbling thunder. It drowned out all other noise except the heartbeat drumming in my ears. Lightning flashes through the tall, curtainless windows were the only illumination in the bare, unfamiliar house. The power was out, the phone dead.

All my senses were overloaded: my skin crawled with gooseflesh, my mouth was dry, my nostrils were filled with ozone and old-house smells. At the first *BANG!* I bolted straight up from protective covers and rolled sideways onto the bare hardwood, groping on hands and knees for my pants. I somehow managed to not break the glass kerosene lamp beside the bed, but it was still useless without the matches I'd stupidly left on the kitchen table.

I moved slowly through the old house between lightning flashes, brandishing my glass-lamp sword, using the brief map of each flash-stored image and the sound of the banging kitchen door for guidance. Finally, I stood nervously in the hallway door, waiting for the next bolt of light before venturing into the kitchen.

I caught most of the scream in my throat when the sharp crack of light came. I was not alone! A man was sitting at the small breakfast table! In the blink of an eye, it was pitch black again!

My action-oriented, hard-wired, right-brain amygdala jerked me backward, believing the intruder was already lunging for me. The same nuclei, buried deep on the left side of my temporal lobe, were instantly processing the stored black-and-white image for details and clues: *legs under table, torso hunched above, hair plastered wet to skull, dripping . . . and eyes . . . looking right at me!*

The right brain moved on to more options: *rush forward to force the issue and maybe gain advantage . . . wait . . . or run?* Before consensus was achieved, a soft, familiar voice shattered the noisy silence.

"Sorry to startle you, Bob. I didn't want to wake you, but I needed a little shelter from the storm and . . . I can't get that damn door to stay shut in this wind."

I slumped against the door frame, nearly dropping the lamp, as the voice instantly relaxed every rigid nerve and muscle. I laughed loudly, my preferred but often inappropriate energy-diffusion tool.

"Del, what are you doing back here? You scared the crap out of me!"

"I was trying to finish mowing that last field on the hill, when . . . the storm caught me. I was closer to your house than to mine."

"Are you OK?"

"Mostly."

"Are the matches there on the table?" I asked.

"Uh, yeah, I guess."

Using his voice and the walls, I felt my way over to the tabletop. "Damn," I said as my fingers found the damp box of useless matches.

Suddenly exhausted as the adrenal rush left me, I felt for the chair and rotated it so I could sit with my back to the wall facing out into the room, knowing there was not enough legroom under the small table. I decompressed from my near-death experience. My heart beat was returning to its normal pace, not influenced anymore by the discordant rhythm of the banging door.

We sat in one of the silent valleys that raging storm lines often spawn, and waited for the next line to wash over us.

"Yeah, you told me about the mowing, but what are you doing mowing at this hour? It's got to be two or three o'clock."

"I just didn't have as much time as I thought," he said.

I thought I understood what he meant. Building any young career involves stress and consumes large acreage in our consciousness; finding time for a personal life is challenging at best. But lately, Del's life had changed exponentially. I knew he was under tremendous pressure.

"I wish I had a towel for you, but I'm a little short on household supplies right now. A blanket is the best I can do."

"I'm fine," he chuckled. "I'm almost drip-dried."

"What can I do, Del? Give you a ride home? I'll do whatever you need."

"I know you would. I've been sitting here thinking about that . . . but this storm will pass, and I'll just leave here and walk home over the hill. Then I'll crash big-time. I don't need to involve you."

"Are you sure? I can make some coffee on the camp stove."

"No, thanks. Go back to bed. I'll prop something against the door when I leave."

"OK."

I don't even remember getting into bed. The comfort of another human being in the house and the crash from my adrenaline rush made sleep come easy.

Del and I were part of the tribe of young, professional, back-to-the-land, counter-culture flower children of the 1960s and 1970s. We were now lawyers, architects, engineers, teachers, builders, and seekers, constructing a community, one farm at a time. We were not the first of our tribe to buy affordable land here on the periphery of horse country, just the most recent. Eight of us, spouses, business partners, family, and friends had recently pooled our resources and signed a contract for 120 acres on the edge of the Bluegrass and adjacent to Del's place.

We knew almost all our neighbors before we moved in, including Del. It was not as many locals speculated—we were not positioning ourselves to grow weed when our college buddy, Gatewood, got elected agriculture commissioner or senator or governor and made it legal; we just wanted a place to raise our families in a circle of like-minded people.

The tribe had already started an organic foods co-op, saved Red River Gorge from becoming a lake, and were gearing up to stop a nuclear plant on the Ohio River. In the everything-is-possible attitude of the day, it didn't seem too presumptuous of us to advertise that our farm would host a powwow on the vernal equinox, well before we actually owned the property.

We saw ourselves as the "good and true" in the broad Zoroastrian world concept of good and evil, truth and falsehood. We were fledgling monotheistic pagans, one with the universe and the Aquarian Age. We were leaving Pisces and entering Aries in the time of the Zoroastrian "New Day" as the sun crossed the equator and balanced light and dark.

Time and the universe were on our side; we could keep chaos

at bay! We did not suppose anything could stop us. If things went on schedule, we would close, take possession, and some of us would be living on the farm a full month before the housewarming party.

The division of responsibilities available to our large owner group meant that the party planning process could easily progress separately and unimpeded by the legal, financial, and paperwork process. The minor issue of ownership did not slow party preparations.

But the schedule began to slip. Legal, title, and bank issues pushed the closing date back and back and further back, right up against the party date . . . when, finally, the stars and energy conduits of the universe aligned in the blink of an eye, and in the time it takes eight people to sign a stack of papers, the deal was done on the day before the big Friday-night party.

The house would stay empty for at least another week as we changed utilities, got the cistern cleaned and water delivered, and took care of the many details of making a hundred-year-old log farmhouse home for some of us.

Luckily, the party was not precedent setting: the potluck format was long established in the old-hippie community. It was one in a series of celebrations our ilk was prone to, merely our farm's first entry into the tribal social calendar that lets few events pass uncelebrated.

The party committee had scouted the grounds and chosen a grassy spot in the pasture field, in front of the tobacco barn, for the fire circle. The ancient but solid old cedar and hemlock structure, a testament to the builder's knowledge of native woods and construction ingenuity before power tools, would serve as the food-serving and beer keg area and provide a contingency option against the unpredictable late-March weather.

Because I had scheduled vacation days on Friday and Monday, I was the advance setup person for the party, the acting Security Chief, and the first owner to spend a night at the farm; for that purpose, I had loaded a bed, mattress, and box spring into the truck that morning.

The weather forecast called for storms to move in on Saturday night, but the crocus and daffodils around the yard fence were basking in the warm sunny breeze of that early spring Friday morning as I started unloading the bed into the front bedroom of the house.

I soon heard the familiar rhythm of a tractor approaching from over the hill and watched as Del, my new next-farm neighbor, drove his 1950s Ford 8N tractor with his new bushhog through the gap in our shared limestone boundary fence, flushing March rabbits in his wake.

Pulling up to the garden gate and shutting off his tractor, Del threw up his hand and said, "Howdy, neighbor."

"Howdy."

He explained that he was "getting ready for a full day of mowing tomorrow," but was looking forward to the party that night and to having us as neighbors, so he was "willing to pitch in and do what needs to be done today to make this party happen."

I gratefully accepted his offer, but before we got started, I wanted to check out the old tractor with its new brush-cutting attachment. Having grown up around farm equipment, I soaked in every detail. The little twenty-three horsepower, four-cylinder tractor was perfect for a small farm, having a three-point hitch for attaching the mower, a hydraulic lift for lifting it, and a power take-off (PTO) shaft for spinning the hinged blades. He took time to explain the overriding clutch he'd installed to keep the torque of the mower from pushing you into a creek or tree or whatever when you're trying to stop. Having torn through a woven-wire fence at the end of a field in my youth, I knew exactly what he was talking about. I commented on the new front tires with the distinctive ridge down the middle. We could already sense the commonality, the synergy of our neighbor-ness.

After the farm-machinery tech talk, we got down to the business of the party. Del and I searched the sheds and outbuildings of the old homestead to find veteran doors to lay across sawhorses in the hallway of the tobacco barn. The ladies, when they arrived later, would cover them with tablecloths for the large spread of food neighbors would bring. Owing to our well-understood timeframe issues, beer, location, and good vibes were all we were expected to furnish this time.

In the chosen pasture-field dining area, just through the barnyard gate and adjacent to a persimmon tree, we placed an eclectic assortment of lawn chairs, blankets, and old church benches (dragged from the barn) surrounding the fire circle. Del and I had carefully constructed the circle with the more-than-plentiful limestone rocks that were the permanent residents of our new farm.

The late morning and afternoon flew by in a blur of good energy, productive collaboration, and herbal allies, as more and more co-owners and friends arrived with supplies for the party. Hours before the appointed start time, the celebration was well underway and rapidly expanding. We munched on homemade trail mix, and iced, tapped, and sampled the keg of beer, the beverage of choice in that era of our lives.

The afternoon was a smoky haze, and before we knew it carloads of more time-conscious guests were negotiating the steep gravel driveway to our new home. The long table doors sagged with a cornucopia of homemade and organic dishes, reflecting a wide cultural diversity. We ate, talked, drank, sang, danced, and played music; life's concert was making a reunion-tour appearance at the old place.

Holding hands in a large circle around the fire, under the new moon on the "New Day," we sent our combined vibrations out into the universe. Time was frozen. How many eons had this ritual been repeated? How many previous lifetimes had we circled this fire and channeled the heartbeat of Mother Earth through our bodies and into these drums? I did not know Del was a musician, but the entire evening he was immersed in the rhythms of a Sri Lankan drum. He was in a trance, obviously talking to the Creator.

The string, percussion, choral, and dance sections began to thin out around eleven o'clock, and finally, in the early hours of the next day, the party came back full circle to just Del and me. Sitting in the pasture-grass circle, warmed by the fire against the front edge of the coming storm front, we were closing down the old day and preparing to welcome in the new.

Those were my thoughts, but Del evidently was not ready to close down the day just yet. He was pounding on the sinhala drum like a madman. I thought I knew what he was doing. The drum was his medicine tool, shifting his consciousness to a sacred place between the worlds, inaccessible except through the drumbeats. He released the beats, letting them vibrate out from his DNA and his spirit, his life . . . everything hanging from them. His pent-up tensions, questions, and prayers passed through the drum into Mother Earth. In the spaces between the beats, he listened for the vibratory reply.

I could only imagine the tension brought by his recent thrust into national scrutiny. Del's picture and name had been all over the news for the past few months. He was the defense attorney in a local murder trial that, at first, looked iron clad for the prosecution . . . but it was not, and it went far deeper than anyone knew.

Partially through luck and partially through inspired investigation, Del had connected enough dots to show that his client had been set up, a patsy for an international drug ring that went deep into local police and politics. He had turned over a big rock, disturbing a local viper's nest, and the snakes of this cabal had squirmed into unimaginable places.

Tonight, Del was in a faraway trance, at one with the beat. I could not keep up with his drumming, nor keep my eyes open. I left him and the drum under the stars and the persimmon tree and went into the old house. I collapsed into the familiar bed in the unfamiliar room. It was a delightful christening of my new home.

The Saturday morning sun came too soon and unimpeded through the high, curtainless windows, waking me long before I was ready. I boiled bottled water for coffee in a camping pan on the camp stove and took a tin cupful with me out toward the barn. Del's tractor was gone and so was the drum.

Owing to the environmentally friendly nature of our guests, there was surprisingly little trash to pick up from the party. I stirred the ashes and raked glowing coals together, close to the rocks on the near side of the circle, before I collected and piled the small unburnt ends of last night's kindling on top. I soon had the fire crackling.

After my coffee, I disassembled the tables in the barn, checked the beer keg, and moved everything back to the approximate location where we'd found it. The wind was picking up, bringing high, fast clouds ahead of the coming storm. I had the farm to myself today; everyone else was occupied.

I sat with my back against the persimmon tree trying to clear my mind and decipher the sights, sounds, vibrations, and nonverbal communications from the night before. I could hear the sound of a tractor coming from over the hill in the direction of Del's place. *Good, he's getting his mowing done.*

The day passed quickly. I went into town to check on a new water heater, get new door hinges, and have a late lunch at a tribal-owned vegetarian restaurant before heading back to the farm. I was tired and in bed before it was fully dark and had been asleep four or five hours before Del came in from the storm. I got several hours of additional sleep after leaving him in the kitchen and going back to bed.

Sunday morning was cloudy and soggy. The rain had moved past, but the electricity was still out. I made coffee, fixed the hinge on the kitchen door, and took a walk. When I got back to the house, the electricity was on and the phone was ringing. It was Julie, one of my farm partners, asking if I'd heard.

"Heard what?"

"About Del," she said.

"What about Del?"

"You haven't!" she sobbed. "Bob, he's DEAD!"

"Dead! How? When?"

"He fell off his tractor and got run over by the bushhog. It mangled his legs. He bled to death out in the field!"

"This morning?"

"No, the coroner said late Saturday evening, they didn't find him till this morning."

"Saturday evening! It couldn't have been Saturday evening. He was . . ." My voice trailed off before I finished the sentence.

"I know," she said. "Friday we were all together at the party and now he's gone. Damn, you just never know do you?"

"No, you don't."

After I hung up, I started questioning my memory, and my sanity! Had it all been a dream? I tried to review the facts, the ones I could still physically and visually verify: the kitchen door was definitely busted, a board most certainly had been wedged against it from the outside, there was no leak above the table, but the matches were wet. Most troubling was the sticky dark spot under the small table, which I chose not to touch.

Sorting fact from fantasy, I came across a strong probability: I was likely the last person to see Del alive . . . and the first person to see him . . . risen . . . or whatever. I shivered at the prospect of the bonds such circumstances often seal between spirits. *Will he visit me again?*

The wake and interment services were life celebrations that vibrated all of us, laying bare our vulnerabilities and our love.

A week or so after the funeral, a disquieting rumor began to circulate. Del had made some very rich and ruthless people very unhappy . . . perhaps it hadn't been an accident.

Curious about the rumor, I decided to take a walk along the boundary fence. *I'm just a landowner walking his fence line. What harm or suspicion could come of that?*

I walked circuitously until I had convinced myself that Del's field was not under surveillance before cautiously approaching the crime-scene tape, still attached to a few upright stakes. This was the spot, a wet weather spring–softened area near the edge of a woods. The indentation of Del's body pressed into the soft earth, the tractor-tire marks on either side of the smooth-bottomed depression, and the dark churned earth beyond where the bushhog had drug him and mangled his legs told the story. Looking at the scene, it all made sense to me.

With a big sigh, I turned to leave as a voice in my head suddenly shouted, "Tire marks!"

The depression under his body should not be smooth! There should have been the marks of those front tire ridges under him! I had to go back and look again. If he had fallen sideways from the driver's seat, he would have fallen off behind the front wheel, on ground already marked by its tire; marks that would not have been completely erased as he was pushed down into them by the fat rear wheels. It would have been impossible for him to fall off ahead of the front wheels! But that's what the marks showed.

I looked closer at the bottom of the depression. *No, the front tire ran over him too!* Someone else was driving the tractor when it ran over him!

The back of my neck tingled as I nervously turned and walked toward my place, looking over my shoulder more than once. I didn't feel safe till I got to the old barn. I sat with my back to the persimmon tree, trying to calm down and gather my thoughts. My other senses sharpened as the edges of vision began to soften in the twilight. I tried to keep the dangerous and disturbing vibrations segregated from the calming vibrations of the tree and the earth as I processed the data and reviewed my options.

One vibration kept breaking through . . . I felt it long before I heard it: a drum. I tensed at first, then as I listened longer I relaxed, knowing what was to come.

Somehow, long ago in my youth, I'd learned to read the subtle vocal tones of hounds as they communicated their progress, direction, and excitement from afar. In the same way, I knew the drum was coming toward me and that it was not threatening. I took deep, purposeful breaths, listening to the beats of my own heart, and waited as the drumming came closer, closer. In front of the barn now, slowing and softening respectfully as it neared.

I was still startled when the beats stopped and the soft edges and distinctive markings of the drum suddenly started materializing from a fog in front of me. I knew the drum had come home to stay. Silence filled all the space around me until something inside my head told me it was my turn to speak through the drum. I reached out and lay my hand on its top, waiting for the vibrations to come.

I jumped when I felt the cold hand gently touch the top of mine. Visions and panic filled my head: *Is this it? Is this the cold hand of death?* I accepted that it might be and relaxed. Instantly the visions came. Simultaneous and overwhelming, multiple scenes played out in my mind's eye. I could tune in to each one without losing track of the others. I heard all conversations, knew all names, dates, and contexts.

In one scene, I was hovering above the field two weeks before, as Rick and Jorge stepped out of the woods with guns aimed, making Del get off the tractor. I saw Rick knock Del to the ground and Jorge drive over the unconscious body, dragging and mangling it with the bushhog.

In a more recent scene, I was in an old war plane, a Douglas A26 Invader that had been heavily modified with upgraded engines, avionics, and extra fuel tanks. I knew, with the coming of the corporate jets, these refitted WWII-era, twin-prop, long-range speedsters, now obsolete as executive planes, were the preferred, cheap, and plentiful drug-smuggling plane of the 1970s. I clearly saw the plane on the ground in Columbia, barely long enough for its pilots to take a leak and have a smoke, before being loaded and refueled for the thirteen-hour trip up the seventy-third Meridian, back to the northeast coast of the US. It was a longer route, out over the Atlantic Ocean, but it had the advantage of being east of the radar stations and airplane patrol routes of the Drug Enforcement Agency.

I knew they were not going back to Kentucky on this trip; they hadn't been there for a couple of weeks and needed to stay away for a while longer. Rick had flown all the way down, while Jorge, his longtime Vietnam tour buddy, had slept. Exhausted now, Rick would catch a few winks on the return flight in a sleeping bag on top of the tightly wrapped and duct-taped bags of cocaine, nearly a half a ton of it, packed evenly and strapped down on the cabin floor.

Rick hadn't seen Jorge climb back in the plane, but hearing the engines start to rev up, he knew he was at the controls and anxious to leave. Rick pulled the side hatch closed and yelled toward the front of the plane, "Take us home, amigo!" He couldn't see Jorge; the entrance to the cockpit was a crawl-through hatch leading up to the flight deck, which was elevated above the cabin floor to accommodate the front landing gear housing.

The engines powered up, the brakes released, and after a bumpy ride on the grass runway they were airborne and on the way home. Rick immediately went to sleep.

The next thing he knew, a lightning bolt of pain shot though his head as it smacked hard against the plane's ceiling. It felt like he was in a washing machine as the plane shook, rolled, and dropped violently in the storm. The cargo was strapped down, but he wasn't.

"Damn, Jorge!" he shouted. "Couldn't you fly around it?"

Then he panicked. *Crap!* He remembered having to fly into a storm to lose a Navy plane on his tail the first time he'd flown this route.

"Is Somebody tailing us, Jorge?" he yelled through the roar of the screaming engines and the storm. There was no reply.

Slowly, from one handhold to the next, banging from side to side, trying to stay upright inside the black and violently jerking aluminum tube, Rick made his way forward. A downdraft sent him crashing against the ceiling again and pushed his stomach into his throat before the straining wings caught an updraft and slammed him back to the deck. His head pounding, Rick worked his way toward the small hatchway near the floor, the only access to the cockpit.

"Jorge! Jorge! Damn it, Jorge, answer me! Is everything OK?" Still no answer, nothing but that drum beat in his head.

Rick braced himself at the cubbyhole entrance and peered up into the back of the cockpit, waiting for the next flash of lightning to take visual inventory of Jorge. The drumming was louder, both inside and outside his head. The beat intensified. Something was about to explode!

Rick reached up to feel for the flight deck, intending to hoist himself up into the jump seat behind Jorge. His grip slipped on something slick on the floor above.

"What the . . . AUUUUGH!" he screamed as a flash lit the cockpit.

Jorge's bloodless, mangled body was slumped forward in the pilot's seat, held up by the shoulder harness. Rick's scream was drowned in the inferno as the grinning, partially scalped skull of Del looked down at him from the jump seat . . . beating a drum!

My hand jerked back instinctively as the ice-cold grip released its hold on mine. I slowly relaxed, back into the sheltering heartbeat of the tree.

Years later, the drum still smells of seawater.

I've Got a Story for You Too

The moment the spear left his hand, Paul knew his life would be forever changed. Time was suspended, or at least slowed down to a single movie frame every few seconds. He didn't just throw it—some primal force, some Roman Legionnaire reincarnation took possession and he threw it perfectly. This was not a casual throw; this was a killing throw.

My God where did that come from? he asked himself.

"*You damn well know where it came from!*" said the Legionnaire.

Paul's internal dialogue rattled on,

What a stupid thing to do! Sure, John was a drunken idiot and had single handedly ruined the fraternity campout, but that didn't warrant a hand-sharpened hickory spear to the center of his brain!

"*The hell it didn't!*" said another, raging voice from deep within.

One minute you were sitting against a tree, facing him twenty feet away. You were furiously whittling on a stick, trying to channel your anger, and the next moment, he shouted some drunken utterance and you snapped. You leaped to your feet and chucked that stick . . . and changed your life!

"It was a helluva throw, wasn't it? I can make that throw all day! I'd do it again," came the rough, proud reply.

Yes, he was an insufferable loudmouth drunk and he really pissed you off when he did that human cannonball dive into the middle of the fishing hole just as the fish were starting to bite, but he wasn't worth ruining your life, spending a big chunk of it in jail for manslaughter or murder.

"Screw the weak little shit. He deserved what we gave him! He had no business dancing around the fire till he was so dizzy he knocked over the cooking pot and spilled the stew. He's lucky we didn't throw him in. We're better off without the scum!"

Paul tried to make sense of the debate raging in his head. *What just happened?* He knew the answer as soon as the question formed in his mind. He had known it for years now. John was a happy, stumbling, laughing, bull-in-a-china-shop drunk, but Paul had someone else hidden inside him, someone old, mean, and angry. The more he drank, the more that other persona took over.

As the slow-motion spear buried its tip a good three inches into the middle of John's forehead, Paul said a prayer and made a promise, a promise to spend the rest of his life as an advocate, for others and himself, in overcoming anger, addiction, and all other mental illnesses. Better or worse, his life was never going to be the same.

The slow-motion movie was over and real time began again. The impact of the missile slammed John's head back against the tree. A surprised, wide-eyed look crossed his face before the weight of the long shaft, settling to the ground between his legs, pulled his head forward again.

"AHHHHHH!" he screamed from his bowed position. Paul didn't move as he watched the knot of fire-lit bodies swarming around the impaled and screaming John. Many drunks were now sober as we ignored Paul and debated what to do. John was still talking, yelling for us to "get it outta me," but no one wanted to pull the stick out.

Ideas and options started to flow. We couldn't get him in a car with that long thing sticking out of his forehead. Someone thought of sawing it off, but we could only find a hatchet. Finally, I took the tractor back to the farm house and found a pair of tree-pruning shears. Back at the site, I was relieved to find John still alive as I cut the spear off as close to his head as I dared, leaving only a few inches sticking out. Resembling a bloody-faced unicorn, John did not seem to be impaired in any way, and most agreed that the newly acquired horn did not hurt his looks that much.

Paul did not go to the hospital with us, but heard the stories later that night back at the frat house. The whole episode would be part of fraternity house legend for many years to come.

The trip to the hospital was eventful. Far from being debilitated or even sobered by the new addition to his head, John was determined to show it off. All the way to the hospital, through a busy downtown and particularly at stoplights, John had hung out the passenger-side window, yelling and banging on the side of the car, calling attention to his adornment. Many souls were led to the church that night, convinced that they had witnessed the face of the devil.

Accustomed as they were to all facets of the human condition, the late-night emergency room staff were still quite taken with John's state. X-rays and CAT scans revealed what most of us already knew: John's skull was as thick as a water buffalo's. The spear had not penetrated his skull, but a good two inches of the point had been splintered, flattened, and splayed backward, creating a multiple fish hook effect that anchored it firmly beneath the skin of

John's forehead. He would suffer no lasting damage other than a small scar.

If the episode did little to change John's life or looks, it had a profound change on Paul's. He left the fraternity, quit drinking, applied for medical school, and started therapy. He'd already figured it out before the diagnosis was delivered: DID, Dissociative Identity Disorder, the new name for Multiple Personality Disorder (MPD). He'd long had memories of places he'd never been and people he'd never met. It all fit. *Crap!*

His was not what they called "cooperative multiple systems"; the two people inside Paul didn't get along at all. But there was a saving grace, and it was big. Evidently, alcohol was the only trigger for his dark side to come out; if he didn't drink, it was silent—still there, but under control. It was beneficial sometimes, giving him insights that non-multiples weren't capable of, but thankfully the angry emotional component, the Legionnaire, never again reared its ugly head. He learned to be careful, even about cough medicine.

Paul eventually got an MD/PhD in Psychiatry and Behavioral Science. It was while he was in med school that he met his soul mate, Linda. They both loved travel and art and both were dedicated to mental health advocacy. Shortly after graduation, they got married. Both went to work in the mental health profession, without Paul ever telling her about the . . . other. Linda never asked about his teetotalling.

Years later, as their professional careers wound down and the kids were all gone, Paul and Linda began to travel overseas on extended vacations. Paul's antenna went up when Linda said she wanted to take him to a special place in Rome; the church of St. Peter in Chains near the Colosseum, where Michelangelo's enormous statue of Moses is housed.

The idea of the Colosseum made Paul nervous. Places had never triggered anything, but this was flirting with fire. He was apprehensive, fearing that this might be too far a reach; the Legionnaire might be there waiting to possess him again.

The first night in Rome, Paul was a mess. He was irritable and couldn't sleep. He either had to go with Linda to the Colosseum or tell her the story. He went. Coming out of the Colosseo subway station, Paul was startled to see, directly in front of him, the ancient temple of blood sport and death. He braced for the Legionnaire's anger, but it never came; actually he felt comfortably at home. A short walk away, inside the church, Paul relaxed and really began enjoying himself. He was even giddy about being able to read many of the Latin inscriptions, not sure if his knowledge came from medical school or a long-forgotten past!

He was particularly moved by the statue, not in the way he had feared at all, but because of the amazing ability Michelangelo had of giving life to cold marble. He had read nothing about this statue of the great saint, but when he saw the short horns coming out of its head just above the hairline, he had a rush of memories—both of Rome and of the night that had changed his life. He and Linda were both solemn and reflective.

Later, at a small café near the Spanish Steps, Paul asked about the horns. Linda explained that ancient written Hebrew had no vowels and that St. Jerome, who had translated the Bible into Latin from Hebrew and Greek, had mistaken a certain word to mean "horn"; thus for twelve or thirteen hundred years, everyone who believed in the unerring accuracy of Jerome's translation (including Michelangelo's papal patron) firmly believed that Moses had horns. It wasn't until the 1700s that it occurred to someone that there could be a different meaning. Depending on what vowels you used and the vocalization, the other meaning was "a ray of light." Since then, Moses has been depicted with a halo instead of horns.

Linda said it was funny that he should ask about that detail, because those horns had played a big part in her life. She explained that in high school she had learned that the statue was one of Sigmund Freud's favorites and that he had visited it every summer. At the end of high school, Linda and some friends had gone off to Europe to find themselves. She was struggling with what to do with her life. She was pulled toward psychiatry, but she just wasn't sure; she needed a sign. She hoped that a visit to the statue that had so influenced Freud might provide some guidance for her. It didn't . . . at least not then.

She was still struggling with the question when, a year or so later while working as an undergraduate volunteer at the university hospital, a sign had been given to her. A drunken frat boy was brought to the emergency room with a wooden stake in his head. It made her think of the statue of Moses and she viewed it as a sign from God or Freud or maybe Michelangelo that she should indeed pursue a psychiatric career.

Paul sat back in his chair for a moment and smiled.

"That was a nice story," he said. "Now, I have one for you!"

Mary

Shane and my wife, Cathy, friends since teaching high school together years ago in Kentucky, had kept in touch. Now that he had a position in the Kingdom of Fife, north of Edinburgh, Scotland, it was a good time for us to visit.

It had been a long trip to get to Balbirnie Park in Glenrothes: an afternoon hop from Louisville to Charlotte, an overnight flight to Dublin, a morning flight to Edinburgh, and finally a forty-five-minute ScotRail ride over the Firth of Forth to the Markinch station, where Shane and his wife, Diedra, met us.

They drove us to their nearby apartment, in what had once been the stable block and servants' quarters of the five-hundred-year-old ancestral home of the Balfour family. The four-hundred-acre estate is now a national park known for its rhododendron, hotel, golf course, and craft center, home to glass blowers, potters, and jewelry makers.

Understanding well the stresses of international jet lag, they took us straight up to our room and left us for a time-resetting two-hour nap. Refreshed, we awoke to smells from their well-equipped kitchen. We went down to see if we could help, and to start filling in the gaps of the intervening years. Taking turns away from meal preparation, they each gave us a tour of the old place, stressing how happy they were to have us and that we should make ourselves at home.

When they asked if we'd found everything we needed upstairs, I asked about the lighting in our bedroom. We had not been able to determine the relationship between the wall switch and the bedside lamp, perhaps a burned-out bulb? They exchanged glances before Shane explained, "Nothing to worry about. It's just Mary's again, she loves the dark!"

Mary! I stifled the question till later.

Over a gourmet dinner paired with several glasses of wine, they elaborated. When they first bought the place five years before, neither of them had believed in ghosts. They developed other, more logical explanations about the occasional occurrences in the house: lights suddenly not working, cabinets and doors opening and shutting, water faucets turning on, and a variety of other things.

"This was, after all, a five-hundred-year-old house, and the grounds had been inhabited for thousands of years; one had to expect a certain amount of that sort of thing."

After dinner, Shane went up to check the circuitry and came back to report that both lamp, lamp switch, and wall switch seemed to be functioning properly for now, but candles and matches were on the nightstand at either side of the bed, should we need them.

Cathy and I exchanged concerned glances.

When we were settled into the living room with aperitifs, I inquired more about the history of the place. They told more stories about their home and finally, with additional prodding and more exchanged glances, they reluctantly gave up their ghosts. Diedra reached over to an end table and carefully pulled out a notebook.

"At first everything was harmless and somewhat amusing," she said. But at the top of the stairs one night, on her way to their bedroom, something "unmistakably and without accident," had tried to cause her harm, pushing her down the stairs and breaking her arm. All amusement now gone, both of them admitted help was needed. They were soon in contact with a local paranormal research group, ghost hunters.

Diedra carefully opened the notebook to a worn, corner-folded page and ran her finger down a list.

Shane explained. "During two years of investigation, research, and countless visits, the group identified thirty-four individual ghosts!" The names and biographical sketches of each, carefully recorded in the notebook, were "part of the deal for their leaving."

The ghosts were a diverse group, equally representing both victims and perpetrators in assorted malevolent acts: murders, suicides, illnesses, injustices, accidents, madness, tortures, and childbirths gone wrong. The painstaking identification process, critical in determining why each of the spirits was hanging around, had to be carefully pieced together and then pried apart. Slowly, one by one, in ways both ingenious, subtle, and sometimes heavy-handed, each of the spirits were, in one way or another, induced to vacate the premises. All except for Mary.

Diedra's finger rested on Mary's name and a smile came to her face. Mary was a bit of an enigma, a mystery. She was a sweet but secretive spirit who delighted in playing simple tricks—electrical circuitry being one of her favorites. Shane smiled and added, "She's particularly fond of male guests. She likes the boys and she likes to flirt!"

"Not to worry, at the most, maybe a soft kiss on your cheek is all."

The afternoon nap and unexpected revelations had helped, but by ten o'clock, Cathy and I were both nodding off in the middle of conservations. We excused ourselves and headed up the stairs to what we hoped would be deep and uninterrupted sleep.

Upstairs, we were relieved when a flip of the switch by the door illuminated both bed-side lamps, but were perplexed when Cathy found her cell phone unplugged. Both of us distinctly remembered her plugging it in before we went downstairs. Perhaps Shane had unplugged it when he came up to test the switch. It seemed plausible. We'd ask in the morning.

We undressed and got into the sheets beneath the soft, light comforter. Cathy immediately switched off her lamp, but I had preparations to make. Before switching my lamp off, I carefully placed the candle and matches on the nightstand. I positioned the candle just to the far side of the lamp, where I wouldn't knock it off fumbling around in dark, and after carefully examining the matches, centered them just in front of and touching the heavy marble lamp base. I practiced reaching over with my eyes closed, recording the distance and position in my mind, feeling for the lamp and its switch, and finally, should they be needed, running my hand down the stand to the matches. Satisfied, I turned out the lamp and pulled up the covers. I was quickly asleep.

Mary came to me softly in a dream, standing beside the bed, looking down at me. I was not alarmed. She liked me. I knew it was a dream, and the vibe was a pleasant and relaxed . . . until I felt the rush of cold air as the covers rose over me and Mary was snuggling in beside me.

"No! No!" I shouted, throwing back the covers, sitting up and groping for the lamp—thankfully, exactly where it should have been. Cathy, miraculously, did not stir. I found the switch and flipped it . . . nothing . . . darkness. As practiced, my fingers hurriedly followed the stem down to the base, feeling for the matches. They weren't there! My hand frantically fumbled around the small table, my heart pounding in my ears, till . . . suddenly, there they were . . . pressed into my hand by another, smaller, cooler hand!

Close into my ear, a soft, warm voice whispered, "Here . . . silly, shy boy!"

D-Day Beaches

We sat in exhausted silence. Tourist season was well past, and Route 8 in front of the bed and breakfast in Merville, France, saw only the occasional Renault. Between us, an empty pizza box and a late-night bottle of Côtes du Rhône sat on the small wooden table near Sword Beach. Things were winding down and we knew it—this night, this trip, our lives—it was time to go home. We had been chasing ghosts in the spots where countless spirits had passed through the vortex.

With the diary of Bob's fighter pilot dad as our guide, we'd started in England, in East Anglia, chasing the ghost of a man neither of us knew, whose last combat flight had been out of Leiston Airfield, the Allied airbase closest to Germany and home to the fabled 357th Fighter Group. The 357th was the first US unit to be equipped with the new American P-51 Mustang fitted with the British Merlin engine. It was the perfect metaphor for wartime synergies, and finally an Allied fighter with enough range to escort the heavy bombers (B-17s and B-24s) anywhere they went and back. No longer could German pilots wait to pounce on the bomber stream just beyond the point where other US fighters, low on fuel, had to turn back. The Mustangs now went ahead of the "heavies" and swept the skies of the Messerschmitts and Focke-Wulfs as they formed up. Nazi Air Chief Hermann Goering later recalled that he knew the war was over when he saw the first Mustangs of the 357th over Berlin.

Released from escort duty after the bombers had dropped their ordnance, the fighters were free to hunt the skies of Europe in search of "targets of opportunity." The Mustang-Merlins of the 357th proved to be the best hunters in the US 8th Air Force; they shot down the most enemy planes (609), had the most aces (pilots with five or more confirmed kills), and shot down the most German jets. Not bad for a propeller-driven airplane.

It was on one of these "hunting" forays in clear skies over Normandy in early 1944 that Bob's father sealed a Messerschmitt pilot into a flaming coffin—the acrid smell of his own burning flesh a last earthly sensation—and moments later suffered a similar fate, courtesy of the dead pilot's wingman.

At the old airfield, now a "caravan park," we found the caretaker, who unlocked the small museum and let us peruse the pages of the old mission logs. The typed entries told only the cold facts of that February day in 1944: the names of pilots, the number of planes that had taken off, the number of enemy aircraft and targets destroyed, and the number of planes that did not come back.

Of particular interest in a display was the uniform of an unlucky Luftwaffe pilot who'd crashed near the airfield later that same year. We took pictures of the sinister black uniform and the distinctive boots, still menacing after seventy years. The boots spoke of the specialized efficiency of the German war machine. They were not the hobnailed jackboot of the German infantry; these were specially designed, lightweight boots with circular rubber discs on the soles, made specifically for climbing across slick metal wing surfaces.

We took pictures standing next to the one-third-scale Mustang model and drove slowly along the narrow, dusty farm lanes, around and across the abandoned five-hundred-acre airfield. We paused to look down the long runway, imaging the sights, sounds, and emotions of Bob's father's last takeoff roll toward Berlin, hoping that a thousand miles and six hours later, he'd be back at the Lion's Hill Free House sharing a story and a draft with his buddies. It was left to us, seventy years later, to have that beer for him, half expecting a young airman in an old uniform to walk through the door.

Leaving East Anglia, we headed south and east to Dover, with a quick stop in Canterbury to search for the headless ghost of Thomas Becket. We hurried on, intent on doing what Hitler thought Eisenhower would: sail across the Straits of Dover to Calais.

Onboard the English Channel ferry, we looked back at the high, white-chalk cliffs, the welcome end-of-mission sight for tens of thousands of Allied pilots, mentioned more than a few times in the dog-eared diary. We had a late lunch sailing through the mist toward France, staying alert for drowning ghosts of the Spanish Armada and for stranded British, French, and Polish soldiers still waiting to be evacuated from the Dunkirk beaches.

In the French Low Countries, in the "fatal avenue," the ancient blood-soaked crossroads of invading armies, we put ourselves in the path of wandering spirits from centuries of grisly warfare: Caesar, Napoleon, William the Conqueror, Guderian, and Patton. The skies above did not bear the scars of the earth below, but we knew it had been no less deadly a place.

We lingered at morning and evening cafés in the La Place

des Héros, the four-acre stone-paved square in the often-fought-over city of Arras. We spent our days exploring Northern France's endless graveyards of industrial slaughter left from the first Great War, our grandfathers' war: Vimy Ridge, Armentieres, and Ypres, where a hundred years before, nearly two million men were killed or wounded, and where Hitler won his Iron Cross.

From the massive and towering Canadian monument on Vimy Ridge, we marveled at the equally imposing white basilica of Notre Dame de Lorette on an adjacent hill, surrounded by the cemeteries, ossuaries, and crypts of the largest French graveyard in the world—another unmistakable landmark for World War II Allied airmen trying to get home.

Later, surrounded by artifacts of the butchery from the quarter million Frenchmen who had died there in 1915 and 1916, we shared lunch with a reunion of French veterans at the small café on the cemetery grounds and read names from row after row of white crosses, wondering what violence had scarred those souls and kept them palpably near.

Leaving the artillery-plowed plains and ridges of Artois, we moved on to the grounds of a more recent ghost factory: WWII, our fathers' war. We drove French farm roads, from the Ardennes to Dieppe, clogged with spirits still desperately fleeing Guderian's Panzers as they slashed across the throat of the British Expeditionary Force, severing it from the rest of France . . . and the world.

We lingered at the beaches of Dieppe, once littered with rotting corpses of Canadians sacrificed in the D-Day dress rehearsal of 1942.

Finally, we came to the D-Day beaches of Normandy.

From our bed and breakfast in Merville, we explored the many museums and monuments in the surrounding countryside, made famous in June 1944: St. Marie Eglise, Bayonne, Carentan, Caen. We walked many of the fifty miles of landing beaches and quietly studied the maps and legends at the American cemetery. Its commanding view of "Bloody Omaha" beach made us somber and grateful. The peaceful, 173-acre National Cemetery is American soil, bought with the mangled bodies of the 9,387 Americans who rest there.

It gave us shivers to think of the thousands of men running, crawling, cussing, praying, and dying across the quarter mile of open, coverless, red-soaked beach, with Germans pouring overlapping metal death down on them: hard-core, hob-nailed German infantry, hidden in the concrete-and-steel high ground, every machine gun a meat saw, spewing twenty bullets and innumerable flesh-bits every second across every presighted inch of ground.

We looked out from the concrete bunker complexes where Germans, armed with every kind of cannon, mortar, flamethrower, and machine gun, had splayed, disemboweled, and roasted the young Americans who dared set foot on Hitler's shore. Brain bits and body parts of thousands of Americans had been strewn across the red, stinking beach.

Now, at the end of our wade through the charnel house of history, we sat exhausted at our night café table on Route 8 and silently communicated our sadness and relief with long, reflective pauses. We wondered about communication between the worlds, if spirits had been stalking us, trying to reach us. Had we been open enough, sensitive enough? Was it time? We'd tried. We'd straddled the violent energy vortex and left ourselves exposed to the noisy tear at the boundary between this consciousness and the next, the gap where we suspected Bob's father lived. Till now, he had not seemed to be interested in us . . . but that would change in a moment.

Bob stared off across the road, his features suddenly fixed and stone-like.

"OK," he said. "Do you see that?"

I looked at the dark line of trees across Route 8, the beginning of the saltwater marshes, at the mouth of the Orne. I studied the dark woods line and finally said, "Yes, I do."

A little relieved, but unbelieving, Bob asked, "What do you see"?

I pointed. "That light thing, there. I can't tell if it's a dead tree or what, but it stands out."

Bob tensed and sat up straighter. "Yes, it's moving. It's coming toward us."

Suddenly, not as ready to see a ghost as I'd thought, I said, "It's just the clouds moving in front of the moon."

Bob didn't relax his gaze. "No," he said, suddenly standing up. "Let's move."

"Where?" I asked, jumping up, tingling with energy.

As if channeling the mantra of beach commanders that morning, Bob shouted, "We can't stay here. We'll die. Move!"

At an angle away from the apparition but toward the beach, side by side, we took long, quick strides across the gravel lot and up the road. Instinctively, we turned into the narrow, deserted path into the dark wood . . . through the door. There was a brief second of relief from terror when we finally came out of the wooded tunnel into the dimly lighted street; but the relief passed in a moment as we took stock of our new position, hemmed between the dark windows of empty vacation homes and the black marshes of the Orne. Unseen eyes followed our every move.

Constantly looking behind us, I tried to break the tension. "The moon and the conditions are the same," I said.

"What conditions?" Bob asked tersely.

"D-Day. It's later in the year, but the conditions are the same: full moon and low tide."

"Great," he said. "Keep moving!" Agitated and afraid, every few steps he looked back.

"What's wrong?" I asked.

"It's following us," he said, breathing heavily. "I can just get a glimpse of him when I turn around."

I could see nothing. I tried to break the tension again. "We're a couple of big American guys, and besides . . . they have gun laws over here." It didn't help.

We passed through a gap in the grass-covered seawall that marked the high-tide edge of the beach, and walked a few yards out onto the hard sand.

Suddenly Bob yelled, "What's that smell? It's just behind us!" and whirled around.

I definitely smelled something: the sickly, ashy smell of burnt flesh.

Suddenly Bob was yelling, "What do you want? Who are you looking for? No, I am not my father!"

He did not know where the words came from, but as soon as he'd blurted them out, he knew it was a lie. He knew his dad was in him, yelling. He also knew his father had finally come face-to-face with the German pilot he'd shot down, with the man he'd killed.

"The war's over!" he said. "It's done! It's time for us both to let go, to go home!"

For long, vibrating seconds we stared into the moonlit beach until eventually our adrenalin-pumped veins, Bob's dad, and whatever was behind us all quieted and left.

"It happened here," he said.

"What happened here?"

"Where the planes went down, both of them . . . in Merville."

"How'd you know that?"

He didn't answer.

Slowly, we turned and walked across the surprisingly wide beach out toward the English Channel. For an hour or more, with only the sound of the sea, we aimlessly wandered miles along the expansive beach where so much death and suffering had occurred. Physically and mentally exhausted, we knew this search was over. We were ready to go home. Without any other navigation points on the dark and featureless beach, we retraced our footprints in the sand until the rising tide finally obscured them. We kept walking east in the cloudy moonlight along the ocean's edge, guessing at which of the several sets of prints to follow inland across the quarter-mile-wide beach. Our anxiety built, knowing that turning inland too soon would take us through the wrong gap in the seawall, dooming us to hours in the dark forests and swamps bordering the estuary of the Orne. Near exhaustion, we finally decided on a likely set leading away from the surf.

We trudged numbly on for an interminable distance, and were beginning to have panicked thoughts of being in a black, endless time warp when we suddenly came upon the unmistakable theater of our confrontation with . . . whatever it was. Relaxing a bit, knowing we were on the right path, we paused and read the story written in the sand.

There was the sudden, frightened, angry whirl where Bob had whipped around to confront the ghost. We were comforted by the humor we knew would eventually be in the telling of this story—until we again took up our trek back toward the seawall. Three yards away, beyond, behind and between our own steps was a third set of prints: crisp, clear boot tracks in the damp, hard sand that stopped just yards behind us. The throbbing blood vessels of a hormone rush came back for an encore. The prints had the distinctive, round disc-shaped bumps of a Luftwaffe boot. They led neither left nor right nor back, but simply stopped—as if whatever had made them had risen up and sailed away on the fresh ocean breeze . . . finally flying home.

Other Dimensions

It was too late now. I was committed and descending! I had blindly stepped off the roof toward the ladder's top rung before I remembered that I was supposed to check it on the way down because I had felt it slip sideways as my foot left it on the way up! There was that tense, *uh-oh* moment before my foot finally found the solid top rung and I climbed safely down to the deck below. It was just one of the many bullets I have sidestepped in my amazingly blessed life. I thought no more about it.

A week or so later, standing beside my convertible in a bank parking lot while waiting for a friend, I surveyed my surroundings. Two empty spaces away, an elderly man and what I took to be his daughter were huddled around the far-side passenger door of an SUV. They were evidently having some difficulty maneuvering a fragile old lady from her wheelchair into the seat. Having aged parents, I had plenty of empathy for the scene.

Scanning downhill across the lot, I admired a row of brightly restored vintage cars. *Probably some car club outing*, I thought. Then I saw the unattended and unnoticed wheelchair heading down the hill.

Assessing the situation, my brain went into hyperdrive as the scene unfolded in slow motion in my mind's eye. The analytical side of me started calculating the route, distance, speed, and slope of the hill. Without encountering any unseen contingencies, I had a chance! Already moving, I dropped my man-bag into the convertible's seat and contemplated the first potential danger: a sharp turn around the back of my car that, if negotiated incorrectly, could wreck my six-decades-old infrastructure. Limiting my initial acceleration until after I had cleared the car, I planted my right leg and pushed off toward the errant geriatric chariot. *Good so far, no pain from my knee.* I was grateful for my knees and grateful that the bank's outside security cameras hadn't recorded a foolish white-headed guy collapsing and rolling across their lot.

I checked left and right for traffic as I took the first long stride away from my car. I could still abort, but now (recalculating the length of my strides, my lungs request for oxygen, and the spring in my thighs) I gauged that I had at least an 80 percent chance of intercepting the fender-crashing, paint-scratching missile.

Now I hoped the cameras were rolling! I saw the image flash on the local six o'clock news. I could hear the crowd cheering from the sidelines as I raced across the lot, feeling comfortable with the rhythm, speed, and length of my stride. I was going to catch it, but how? I could still buckle a knee if I tried to stop too quickly. Instead, I grabbed the near handle of the wheelchair with my right hand, making a small initial alteration to its course—away from the line of antique cars—and slowing its momentum until both it and I were comfortably in control again.

I did it, without injury, and I'm not even breathing that hard! How good am I?

I turned to face the cheering crowd . . . but . . . there was no audience. Unbelievably, the father and daughter still had their backs toward me, still preoccupied with the mom. The cameras seemed equally unimpressed.

I pushed the wheelchair back behind them and waited to be acknowledged. They were oblivious! I stood there for long seconds, sure that they'd turn around soon. Nothing! Finally, my internal dialogue told me, *OK, I don't really need praise. I proved to myself that I could do it, and now it's done.* I was pleased with myself, and I had helped someone; whether they knew it or not, that was enough.

I set the hand brakes on both wheels and walked back around behind their car and over to mine, still sort of expecting them to notice something. As I got back to my convertible, they finally broke the huddle and the old guy got in the back seat behind his wife. The daughter turned and found the chair exactly where she had left it. She unlocked the brakes without remembering that she had not set them, and wheeled the chair to the rear of the SUV before folding and hoisting it into the now-opened lift gate. Without making eye contact, she got in and drove away!

Calming down, I reflected. *They don't know . . . they'll never know! A tree just fell in the forest and no one heard. This is just too freaky not to mean something. Had those people been real or, needing to manufacture some late-mid-life heroism, did I make the whole thing up? Was it a fantasy, an LSD flashback? Could they really not have seen me? Am I invisible? Did it really happen or not? What am I supposed to learn from this?*

I was still thinking about it a week later when a neighbor knocked on my door. He knew I'd worked for an electronics security company and he wanted to ask me some questions about camera systems. He was thinking of installing one. I invited him in and offered to show him what I had installed, thinking maybe that would help. I showed him the cameras, the wiring, and the recording system I'd set up. He asked how much storage capacity I needed for all those cameras recording around the clock. I explained that the cameras were equipped with infrared detectors and the system only saved the data from a camera if the detector sensed something. I pulled up video from the deck camera to show him. I rewound the system to the previous week. As often happens while trying to demonstrate a point you've just made about equipment, something was amiss. The image of my ladder popped up on the screen, tilted dangerously away from plumb, balanced *en pointe* on a single foot. Shocked, I said nothing. He studied it a moment and asked the obvious question: "I thought you said it didn't record unless there was motion?"

As if on cue, the ladder slowly straightened itself just before my foot came into view from above.

"It must have picked up the motion of me on the roof," I said, not believing it. Thankfully, he did not ask the other obvious question: Who or what had straightened that ladder?

After a few more questions about my availability for later consulting, my neighbor left. I searched the video over and over, trying to find even a single frame of my guardian angel, wondering, *What would I find if I looked at the recordings from those bank cameras?*

Recycling

I almost never go to garage sales or auctions, but this one drew me in. I was back in Western Kentucky, taking my dad's old Lincoln on a drive down memory lane over the roads of my childhood, the narrow, "chat" paved roads leading down to the Ohio River. The cars and trucks parked on both sides left only the narrowest of paths between them, reminding me of Irish roads. I folded in my side-view mirrors before attempting the passage.

A rush of memories came as I paused momentarily at the driveway to the old house and glanced at the crowd gathered in the yard. It was the old home place of one of my childhood buddies, Kevin.

A part of me said, *Keep going, you've put that memory behind you*, but after finally getting past the narrow canyon of cars, another stronger part made me pull over close against the ditch and walk back, into the crowd in the yard, most of which I knew, had known, or knew of. The latter category was comprised of the children and grand- or great-grandchildren of people I'd grown up with. I eventually recognized the auctioneer as Chipper, a not-so-well-aged high school classmate.

It hadn't surprised me when I got news a few months before that Kevin had ended his last days in a prison cell. I could never keep track of whether he was in or out, but the duration of his "outs" had grown progressively shorter. I thought I remembered that the last time he got "sent away" was for a bar brawl in which he shoved a broken beer bottle into someone's face, blinding an eye; that was while he was on parole for that "stolen property thing." *Yeah, that was it.* I'd long realized there was more than one person inside that boy.

Kevin and I had known each other our entire lives. We grew up in Baptist Sunday school together, and until about the fourth or fifth grade we were best buddies—but that's when a different Kevin showed up, an aggressive, smart-mouthed showoff and bully who quickly assembled a gang of eagerly compliant miscreants to back him up.

Overnight, our relationship became confrontational at every meeting. I had to be careful at recess lest he approach me with an earnest look, as if to tell me something of importance, only to suddenly flash that maniacal grin and push me backward over one of his maladjusted scoundrels, positioned on all fours behind me. If I left my bike unattended while they were around, flattened tires would be the easiest I got off.

As teens, our bicycles were our most prized possessions, extensions of our developing personalities. I had a classic Schwinn touring bike with chromed front and back carriers, a tank horn, dual headlights, and handlebar streamers. Kevin had a highly customized, wheelie-popping dragster with high-rise handle bars. I was never able to catch him in the act, but he and his crew were always "just leaving" when something bad happened to my bike. Kevin was always out front, pulling a celebratory wheelie and looking back at me with that evil grin.

Only once did we have an honest and civil conversation during that period. It was at the Homecoming Sunday on the Grounds dinner at our church with both our extended families present, where he knew the gratification that he would garner from any mischief would not be worth the consequences. He was evil, but not dumb. We were seated beside each other at a large outdoor table under the shady grove of hickory trees surrounding the church. In that relatively safe environment, and at a moment when those seated close enough to hear had gone back to the long food table for seconds or desserts, I asked in a low voice without looking up, "Kevin, we used to be friends. What happened to you?"

He paused a moment. As I turned toward him, I saw that evil grin slowly transform his face and he said, "You don't know who I am anymore, do you? You haven't figured this out yet. I like that!"

"No," I said. "But I will, and you won't like it when I do."

Less than a week after that, as I rode my bike into the gravel parking lot of Granny's store I saw the bicycles of Kevin's gang strewn around the big front porch. Instead of pulling around back and putting my bike safely in the store's tool room and coming in the back door (as had become my habit in such circumstances), I parked my bike alongside theirs on the front porch. After a few moments, I went into the store just as "the gang" was coming out the big double doors with the Eat Bunny Bread logo sprayed into the screens. There were snickers and sideways glances as we passed.

Once inside the store, I was in no hurry to get back out to the porch. I knew what was happening. When I did come back out with a cold drink and a candy bar, they were "just leaving." I sat down on the old bench and looked over at my bike. The chain was off, both tires were flat, and the seat was turned around backwards. I calmly watched as they headed off down the road toward the river and then circled back for the gloating pass in front of the porch, with Kevin at the lead in a tight V for Victory formation.

Predictably, with a practiced jerk of the handlebars, Kevin popped a wheelie. With the bike's front end in the air, Kevin looked back over his shoulder at me with that snide grin. I watched closely and saw it in his eyes the moment he first realized something was amiss. He turned his pointy head forward and down toward the bike's front fork, where the front wheel was supposed to have been attached, but was not. The wheel had a slight a lead on him, wobbling off down the road, unattached.

Before his troglodyte mind could grasp the situation, his vacant front fork had ploughed deep into the rough roadway, causing a spectacular five-bike crash with Kevin at the bottom of the tangled pile. His trajectory was forward and down through his handlebars, rasping numerous body parts on the newly laid, knife-edged, limestone-tar-and-rock pavement. Karma was clearly at work as a twisted handlebar caught him squarely in his privates and the rest of the rat pack slammed into a heap on top of him.

Putting down my drink, I sauntered out to the pile in the road and waited patiently for Kevin to emerge from the bottom of the twisted, tangled mass of bikes and bodies. He was a crying, sobbing mess; one side of his face looked like ground beef embedded with rocks, both of his pants legs were ripped away, exposing bright road-rash knees, and the palms of his hands were gouged and shredded.

"Are you alright, Kevin?" I asked, as I offered my bandana handkerchief. I think your front axle nuts must have come loose. I'm sure I can figure this out and fix it for you. I just happen to have the right sized wrench here in my pocket."

Addled, he stared at the wrench stupidly.

With a grin, I said, "You don't seem to be yourself, and you don't know who I am, do you? You'll figure it out!"

Through the rest of middle and high school, Kevin and I had little interaction. Once I went off to college, I never saw or heard from him again except through secondhand stories from relatives and friends in the area. Sometimes when I heard of his domestic or legal troubles, I'd get copies of local papers to read the sanitized but still disturbing details.

With Kevin's passing, the last heir was now gone and his parents' old home place, with all its contents, was being auctioned to pay creditors. The weathered house and the jumbled junk on sale in the yard told the story of Kevin's twisted life journey. There were few things that had much heart or life left.

As I scanned the motley collage of his belongings, I paused at the old bike frame. *Really?* It was at once abhorrent and attractive to me. *Why would I want that thing?* I mused. I couldn't come up with a reason, but I wanted it. There wasn't much left: the front wheel was missing (*Such irony*, I laughed), the chain was broken, the handle bars were twisted, and the back wheel was only held to the frame by the coaster-brake bracket.

I caught Chipper's eye and said, "Five bucks for the bike?"

"Sold," he nodded and grinned.

I wasn't sure if I was happy or sad, or why I'd bought it in the first place. I brushed it off and managed to fit the bike in the huge trunk of my dad's old Lincoln. Back at home in Louisville, I didn't have a place in my mind or my garage designated for it. My expedient impulse was to put it over in a corner, out of sight until I could figure out what to do with it.

I went into the house trying to examine my motivation for bringing the artifact home. Later in the evening, thinking a rustle in the garage had to be Jasper, our hound dog, coming through the doggy door and getting into the recycle bin again, I opened the garage door, flipped on the light, and stepped onto the landing. The bike was in the middle of the floor, facing the wall and the old store bench that I'd saved from the front porch of the grocery before it was torn down in the early 90s, a treasured artifact of my youth.

At first I was stunned, then, as I'd hoped it would, the revelation came in a flash. I knew why I'd brought the bike home. It had asked me to bring it home! I closed the door, walked down the steps, and sat on the old bench directly in front of the wreck. It was the ghost relic of unanswered questions about our divergent lives' flow.

"OK," I said. "It's time we talk."

A chill suddenly came over the room and the overhead light flickered.

"The dark was always your ally," I said as I got up and switched off the light. Back on the bench, moonlight came in through the window and winked at me from the patches of chrome still left on the handlebars. I paused, gathering well-worn questions from the dusty files in my brain. Finally, I said, "What happened to you? There was a time when we were buddies, we understood each other, and then you went off in a different direction and never came back. What happened?"

A cloud of restless vapor formed around the derelict frame, changing shape, dissipating and reforming in a troubled, restless swirl. The cloud had a voice, maybe only in my head, but it was loud and clear.

"Hate," it said. "When my temper came up, it took over, made me different, gave me power, made me feel strong. People paid attention to me, admired me. Anger was better than any drug I ever took, and I liked it . . . a lot! I got to where I didn't wait for things to make my temper explode. I called it, manufactured it, lit my own fuse, just for the hell of it, just for the rush."

"It didn't serve you well," I said.

"No, I guess not. But after a while it was all I had, all I knew. I just went with the flow."

"We're all in the same flow," I said. "But you got pulled into different currents. We followed different spirit advice I guess." After a pause, I knew the answer. I'd finally figured it out! "You never ate the beans your grandma gave you, did you?"

There was no answer.

In the morning, I took the twisted relic down to the river, to the big recycling center.

Acknowledgments

Without the love, patience, and watchful eye of the old spirits of the nearly forgotten community of Ragland, Kentucky, this book would not exist.

Thanks to the support of my loving family: my English teacher wife Cathy, our son Ian, who continues to inspire stories, and Granny Parker, who kept the front porch light burning bright. To Roberta Brown for believing in me and pushing me to do what I always wanted, to Lee and Joy Pennington for teaching me the nuts and bolts of storytelling, to John Gage who gave me a radio show front porch to keep me writing stories, and to Ruthi Martin, a friend since high school, who avidly read and reread each version of every story.

This book is for all my kindred spirits, whose stories tie us all together.